EYES OF A STALKER

A SHELBY BELGARDEN MYSTERY

EYES OF A STALKER

Valerie Sherrard

A BOARDWALK BOOK
A MEMBER OF THE DUNDURN GROUP
TORONTO

Editor: Barry Jowett
Proofreader: Rochelle Blaak
Design: Alison Carr
Printer: Transcontinental

Library and Archives Canada Cataloguing in Publication

Sherrard, Valerie
Eyes of a stalker / Valerie Sherrard.

"A Shelby Belgarden mystery".
ISBN 13: 978-1-55002-643-6
ISBN 10: 1-55002-643-7

I. Title.
PS8587.H3867E94 2006   jC813'.6   C2006-904262-4

1   2   3   4   5   10   09   08   07   06

 Conseil des Arts du Canada   Canada Council for the Arts   Canadä   ONTARIO ARTS COUNCIL CONSEIL DES ARTS DE L'ONTARIO

We acknowledge the support of the **Canada Council for the Arts** and the **Ontario Arts Council** for our publishing program. We also acknowledge the financial support of the **Government of Canada** through the **Book Publishing Industry Development Program** and **The Association for the Export of Canadian Books**, and the **Government of Ontario** through the **Ontario Book Publishers Tax Credit program** and the **Ontario Media Development Corporation**.

Printed and bound in Canada
Printed on recycled paper

www.dundurn.com

Dundurn Press
3 Church Street, Suite 500
Toronto, Ontario, Canada
M5E 1M2

Gazelle Book Services Limited
White Cross Mills
High Town, Lancaster, England
LA1 4XS

Dundurn Press
2250 Military Road
Tonawanda, NY
U.S.A. 14150

For Andrew & Shelley
with much love.

CHAPTER ONE

Grade eleven! All through the years — and right up until now — it's seemed as if school would just keep going on and on — like that cute pink bunny in the commercials. Then, all of a sudden, it's the year before graduation and whole weeks are just sliding away like crazy.

The main reason time seems to be zipping past might be that my boyfriend, Greg Taylor, is in grade twelve this year. I try not to think about it too much, but once in a while it's impossible not to wonder what it will be like next fall, when I'm in my last year of high school, and he's away somewhere at university.

I mentioned this to my best friend Betts once, but she wasn't exactly a comfort. All I'd been thinking about was how little Greg and I would see of each other. Betts had a whole different slant on it.

"I guess you're worried about him being around all those university girls, huh?" she said sympathetically.

"Not really," I said. "I was just …"

"It's like a whole new world out there," Betts said, cutting me off. "No parents looking over your shoulder at every last thing you do. No curfew. No rules. Just parties … and freedom. It's almost enough to make me think about going myself."

"Betts, that is *not* what university is about," I said, but I was already picturing throngs of party girls throwing themselves at Greg.

"And co-ed dorms," she went on, like I hadn't spoken at all. She had a happy, faraway look in her eyes. "Just imagine."

"Betts! We were talking about how I was going to miss Greg," I snapped.

"Oh, uh, yeah. Sorry." She offered a crooked smile and then tried to look sympathetic. "Of course, Greg wouldn't get into any of that stuff."

This last comment on the subject was delivered with such a complete lack of conviction that I thought I'd better let the whole thing drop. Betts isn't always that insensitive, but she'd recently broken up with Derek, a guy she'd been seeing for a while, so her views on relationships were a bit sour. I cut her a little slack.

So … where was I? Oh, yes — early into grade eleven. In fact, it was the last week of November, long after I'd settled back into the routine of homework and studying and all that stuff, which is always an adjustment after summer holidays. One thing that was different about this year was that I knew my marks were going to count toward university entrance, so I'd made up my mind not to slacken after the first burst of energy wore off, like I usually do. So far so good with that.

I'd considered getting a part-time job for the school year, but in the end I decided against it. For one thing, my parents thought I should concentrate on school (because of the marks, as I just mentioned), but I also wanted to enjoy the last couple of school years before heading off to university.

It didn't take long for me to be glad I wasn't working! I'd never have had time to do some of the other things I got involved with this year. I usually didn't get involved in extracurricular activities, unless you count volleyball — that's the only sport I was ever any good at — but I'd kind of lost interest in it, too. So, it looked as though it was going to be a pretty laid-back year outside of regular class stuff.

Then I joined the drama club. I almost didn't; the idea of performing in front of a bunch of people didn't appeal to me that much. But Betts talked me into it. Not that Betts herself is particularly keen on drama, but she's definitely interested in one of the guys who's into it.

Like I said, Betts and her boyfriend had broken up, so she was doing what she always did under those circumstances: looking around for someone new. Betts doesn't like being unattached for very long.

Anyway, she'd decided that Kevin Montoya would make a suitable boyfriend, which happens to be an idea shared by a lot of girls in Little River High. In fact, the drama club would have had a lot more members this year, except for the fact that Kevin's name wasn't on the sign-up list during registration week.

There are sheets for the different clubs posted outside the office at school during the second week of September, and you can't get in later on unless you have a legitimate reason for missing the registration period. Kevin had been out sick and had missed the registration, but since he had a good excuse he was able to sign up the next week. But because he was late joining, all the girls who *would* have signed up for drama when they saw his name on the list missed out.

Except for Betts, that is. She'd overheard him and his best friend, Edison Hale, talking about what they planned to join when she was behind them in the cafeteria line-up.

"This is *so* meant to be," she'd told me in her usual excited way. "It's like fate is putting us together."

Then she'd got that dreamy look that told me there was no sense in talking for the time being. Betts was off on one of her happy fantasies, eyes drifting and mouth just slightly turned up at the corners, like a smile had got stuck halfway onto her face.

I wondered what her chances were of snagging Kevin, fate or no fate. She had a lot of competition, and no one had pinned him down yet. He dated a lot, but never the same girl more than a couple of times.

Kevin used to be one of those guys no one paid much attention to: a bit chubby and babyish looking right up until last year. Then he must have started working out or something, because he got in really great shape. It was like everything about him changed with the new look, even the way he walked and talked. Girls started noticing him big time.

Anyway, all of that aside, the bottom line was that Betts pestered and begged and finally dragged me with her into the drama club.

There were seventeen of us in the club, not counting the teacher who organizes it — Miss Lubowski. She teaches grade twelve English, wears high heels and skirts, and drives a really cool car. (A guy could probably tell you what kind of car it is, but all I know is that it's black and sleek.)

I'd expected most of the drama club to be girls, so it was a surprise to find that it was almost evenly divided, with nine girls and eight guys. It would have been nine and nine if I'd been able to persuade Greg to join, too. He said there was no way he'd have time for learning lines and rehearsals and all that stuff.

Greg did join one club this year, though, and I signed up for that with him — but only because I was honestly interested myself. The club was a book club, but was a bit different than most. It was more like a combination book and writing club, and a local author joined us some weeks. On those nights, he'd talk about writing, give us tips, and have us do little assignments and stuff. I'm not going to tell you his real name because he always insisted he liked to keep a low profile. I'll just call him Webster.

The book club was small and predominantly female. Besides Greg and me there were seven other girls and four other guys for a total of thirteen students. (A few of the kids were also in the drama club, which makes sense since both clubs are about stories in one form or another.) Then there was the teacher, Mr. Grimes, and, when he could make it, Webster.

It didn't take long to see that there was going to be a little conflict between Mr. Grimes and Webster. It started pretty much the first time Webster joined us, and kind of took over.

Not that Mr. Grimes was exactly the group's leader or anything. He really tried to stay in the background and just offer comments or help if we asked for it. But the way Webster jumped in and took over, kind of assuming centre stage and acting like he was the single and sole authority on all things written, well, that got under Mr. Grimes's skin pretty fast.

I remember how taken aback I was the first time this happened. It was right after Ellen had shared a short piece she'd written with the group. When she was finished (and after we all clapped, because we always do that after someone is brave enough to read their work) she looked around shyly, waiting for some feedback.

It was then, during the usual pause (when everyone was trying to think of something to say) that Webster pounced. He leapt to his feet and wrung his hands, pacing back and forth with this strangely anguished look on his face.

"No, no, no, child!" he cried, turning to meet Ellen's startled eyes. "Your sentences are loose in places and tightly bound in others. And you've used several words that, quite frankly, do not fit what you're trying to say!"

It's hard to know how much more he'd have said, but for Grimes getting to his feet and clearing his throat. Webster paused, his hand stopping on its upward journey to some kind of artistic gesture.

"Our focus is on creativity, not syntax," Grimes said in the mildest possible manner. Mr. Grimes is a quiet man, not the sort you could picture in any kind of disagreement, so it was a bit surprising that he spoke up at all. Still, I've seen him become quite impassioned about literature in class, so I guess there's depth there that you wouldn't see under normal circumstances.

Anyway, from that moment on there was an undercurrent between the two men. Nothing really overt, but you could sense tension between them at times, especially in the way Mr. Grimes would stiffen ever so slightly whenever Webster walked into the room.

I may have been the only one who even noticed the animosity, but I watched it with interest. I'd been thinking that I'd like to study something related to human behaviour after I finish high school, with the idea of going on to work in law enforcement and eventually becoming an investigative profiler.

I couldn't know that what was about to happen would convince me once and for all to either follow that dream or give it up forever.

CHAPTER TWO

The first meeting of the drama club had almost been enough to make me quit! Ms. Lubowski started off by announcing that we were all going to try out for a leading part in one of the plays the group would be performing over the school year.

"Not everyone will get a leading role," she said with a bright smile, "but it will help me to see your strengths and cast each of you in a part that's suitable."

The thought of getting up on the stage and doing even one scene in front of the whole group was enough to make my stomach queasy, and I told Betts as much while we gathered books from our lockers afterward.

"So? Just make sure you don't get a part." She shrugged in a way that told me she'd already figured that out. "I don't want to be in any stupid play either.

Unless, of course," she smiled and her eyes lit up, "I was starring in a romantic role with Kevin."

"You told me we could just sign up and ask to work on lights or scenery or something," I said, ignoring the way she'd changed the subject.

"Yeah, well, when they see how lousy our acting is, we'll be lucky to be assigned to parking cars on performance nights. Just relax. No one's going to cast you as Queen Macbeth or anything."

"Lady," I said. It didn't surprise me that Betts had it wrong, even though we'd taken that play last year. English isn't her best subject, and Shakespeare isn't exactly easy.

"Huh?"

"It's *Lady* Macbeth. And anyway, I wouldn't even play her for a tryout. She was horrid."

"Yeah, you're right. I remember she was mean. Bubble, bubble, double trouble," Betts chanted. "Burn the stew and ... uh, I forget the rest."

"You forget more than 'the rest,'" I laughed. "It's 'Double, double toil and trouble; fire burn, and cauldron bubble.' But anyway, that's not Lady Macbeth, it's the three witches. Ms. Lubowski said we had to do something from one of the main characters."

"Well, there are other plays to pick from," Betts said. "What did she say they were again?"

"There's *A Doll's House* or *Glass Menagerie*." I

sighed. "I wish she'd picked at least one play that isn't depressing."

"I thought plays were *supposed* to be depressing," Betts said.

"That's because the only ones we ever take are so gloomy. Maybe they think we'll learn more from them than we would from something funny and happy, but this is different. It's a club, not a class. And I bet we'd sell more tickets to something cheerful."

"Such as?" asked a voice from behind me. I spun around and discovered that it belonged to Ms. Lubowski. My face instantly began to burn.

"I, uh ..."

"Really, Shelby, I'm interested." She smiled, but her smiles are always hard to read. "Our play schedule is hardly written in stone. If you have an idea for something different, I'd be happy to consider it."

"Or, we could vote," Betts said.

"Vote?"

"Yeah, like, let the group decide what plays to do."

"Well, that's certainly a thought," Ms. Lubowski said. She did a good job of hiding any enthusiasm she had for that idea, and she turned back to me almost immediately. "So, did you have something specific in mind?"

"Not exactly," I admitted. "At least, not yet."

"Well, think it over. Our next club meeting isn't until Thursday, so if you bring something to me by

Wednesday I'll have time to think it over." After a pause she added, "And, of course, I'll give some thought to your suggestion as well, Betts."

At home later that evening, I wondered why I hadn't just kept my opinion to myself. I knew nothing about plays and couldn't come up with a single idea for one the drama club could perform, no matter how hard I thought.

It was Dad who rescued me, though I might not exactly have deserved it. He'd come into the TV room where I was sitting with Ernie, our newly adopted cat, and clicked on the set. This did nothing to help me concentrate, and it startled Ernie so that he jumped down, scratching my arm in his panic.

I glared at Dad.

"Now there's a happy face if ever I saw one," he said. Dad is a good guy, but sometimes he has the sensitivity of dust.

"I was *trying* to think," I said.

"Ah ha! I thought I smelled something burning."

"Aren't you just the master of wit," I mumbled. (There's no reason to go overboard with the enunciation when you're being rude to your parents.)

It doesn't matter, though. If they don't hear you the first time — and it's amazing how often they *do*, no matter how indecipherable you are — they're sure to make you repeat yourself.

In this case, there was no need for repetition. Dad raised an eyebrow (never the best sign with him) and very deliberately lifted the remote and clicked the TV off.

"Care to tell me what's making you so charming at the moment?" he asked.

"Sorry," I muttered.

"I didn't ask for an apology," he said, "not that it wasn't due. I asked what the problem was."

"Betts made me join the stupid drama club," I said crossly. "And now we have to try out for a part in front of everyone, which I don't want to do. And on top of that, I said something that the teacher over-heard about the plays being depressing, and now I have to come up with one that isn't. Only I don't know any."

"Seems like a good reason to snap at your father," he said, nodding.

"I said I was sorry. And anyway, you were annoying me."

"Well, take me out and pistol-whip me," he said. Dad says weird things sometimes. "Anyway, I might be able to help."

"Yeah?"

"Your mother and I saw a very comical play a few years back: *The Americans are Coming* by Herb Curtis."

"I've heard of the book," I said. "You mean it's a play too?"

"Well, almost any novel can be done as a play. It's a matter of someone writing it in the right format for the stage."

"And that's already been done for *The Americans are Coming*," I said, "since you and Mom saw it. It would be perfect!"

A loud meow sounded and I looked around to see Ernie peeking at me accusingly from the corner of the doorway. I scratched invitingly on the couch and he came toward me, but veered off at the last second and walked past, head high. He does that when he's suffered some imagined kitty injury — mostly to his pride — just to make sure no one thinks he cares.

"C'mon now, Ernie," I coaxed while he sniffed the air indifferently. "No one meant to upset you."

He looked at me, his usually bright eyes lazy and bored. After pausing to yawn and stretch he made his way back to the couch and leapt up. It was pure performance — Ernie's usual act of total disinterest — and I could hardly keep from laughing. I just managed to suppress it because I knew he'd get all indignant and insulted and have to be sweet-talked all over again.

"That rascal is spoiled beyond redemption," Dad commented.

"He sure is," I said pointedly, looking straight at him. This time it was my turn to raise an eyebrow. He looked away pretty quick.

He can say what he likes about Ernie, but Dad is about the worst offender when it comes to spoiling the little guy. He tries to cover it up, but I've caught him sneaking Ernie bits of haddock off his plate and covering for him when he's been on furniture that's supposed to be off limits. I've even seen him carrying Ernie in under his jacket if it starts to rain when the cat's outside.

Even though Ernie's only been here for a short time, it's hard to imagine our house without him.

He snuggled down on my lap, purring happily while I stroked his silky black fur. That's one thing about Ernie. He might be all aloof for a few minutes, but he's really quite forgiving.

Unless there's a second disturbance, which can send him off sulking for hours. And that's what happened only a few moments later when Mom called out for me to come to the kitchen.

CHAPTER THREE

While Ernie pranced off, head in the air and tail snapping, I hurried to see what Mom wanted. As I got to the kitchen doorway I could see that she wasn't alone. Her back was to me and she was talking to a man at the door.

"Shelby, honey, there's a delivery for you," she said, turning her head, when she heard me approaching.

"A delivery?" As Mom moved aside I saw that the man was holding a large plant that had been done up in cellophane.

"Yes, ma'am." The man smiled and held the plant out toward me.

I took it and sat it on the table, signed the delivery slip, told him "thanks," and closed the door.

I clipped the ribbon that was tied at the top and gasped as the cellophane fell away to reveal the most gorgeous plant I'd ever seen.

"A calla lily!" Mom said. "It's beautiful!"

"Is there a card?" I asked, peering in among the leaves. At the same time, I tried frantically to think if today was some kind of special occasion for Greg and me. He'd sent me flowers before, but it wasn't a regular thing with him. Sometimes he'd show up for a date with a rose or carnation, but nothing like this.

"The card is attached to the ribbon," Mom pointed out.

I saw it then, and opened it quickly, still curious and unable to think of an explanation for the delivery. The tiny card matched: pale lavender with a calla lily along the side. Its message was short: *"You will always be mine."*

Mom was standing there, pretending she wasn't waiting to see what kind of romantic message Greg had put on the card. I read it out loud so she could stop trying so hard to look uninterested.

"You will always be mine?" she echoed.

"That's all it says." Something uneasy stirred in me, but it disappeared as soon as I looked at the lovely plant again. "I can't think of why he'd be sending me this. It's not any kind of anniversary that I can remember."

"It's a bit of an odd thing to write on the card," Mom commented. "Of course, I'm sure he meant it to be romantic." She forced a smile.

"It must *mean* something," I said, "only I can't think what."

"I hope so," Mom said. "Otherwise it has an awfully possessive tone to it."

"Well, I'll give him a call right now and find out." I gave her a look and she took the hint and left the room. It's kind of a compromise we've reached that if I want privacy for a phone call, my folks will try to give it to me, since they keep turning me down when I ask to have a phone in my room.

I dialled Greg's number and he answered right away.

"What's up?" he asked. His casual voice sure wasn't giving anything away.

"I just wanted to thank you for the beautiful plant," I said. "Was it for, uh, a special reason?"

"What plant?"

"The plant you sent me." Was this some kind of game?

"I didn't send you a plant."

"What?"

He repeated himself, not that I hadn't heard him perfectly well the first time. I stood there holding the phone, trying to sort out this new bit of information.

"But if it wasn't you …"

"Yeah, that's what I was just thinking." His voice was light and teasing, though. Greg knew he had nothing to worry about from any other guy. I'm crazy about him.

"Then who?" I finished the question automatically.

"There's no card or anything?"

"Oh, there's a card all right, but there's no name on it." I told him what it said.

"That's creepy." The breezy tone was gone. He sounded almost angry.

"To tell the truth, I found it a bit creepy even when I thought *you'd* sent it," I admitted. "I just figured it meant something, and once you told me what it was it would make sense."

"What kind of plant is it?"

"It's, uh, some kind of lily." I found the information spike in the soil and pulled it out. "A calla lily. Why?"

"I dunno. I just thought maybe it signified something. Like certain colours and types of flowers are supposed to mean certain things. What colour is it?"

"White."

"I don't even know why I'm asking these things," he said. "It's not like I'm some kind of expert on what any of it means. Do you know?"

"Not really," I said. "But it's not likely that whoever sent it knows either."

"Well, it's strange, that's for sure. But I'm sure he'll identify himself to you before very long."

"I guess you're right," I said. That thought didn't exactly make me feel better. I could picture how awkward it would be having some guy come up and tell me he'd sent the plant. What would he be expecting? That I'd dump my boyfriend for him because of a plant?

We finished talking and I went back to the TV room.

"So, did Greg explain what the message meant?" Mom asked.

I told her what I'd found out and she turned to my dad right away. "Randall, maybe we should look into this. I don't like it."

"I doubt it's anything to worry about," Dad said. "Anyway, what can I do? We don't even know who sent it, but it's a safe bet that it's just some kid with a crush on Shelby."

Mom wasn't convinced. She went to the kitchen and called the flower shop to see what she could find out about the sender, but when she came back it was without any answers. She still looked worried.

"They said it was a mail-in order, paid for in cash, with no return address or anything. And they didn't even keep the envelope or paper with instructions."

"Then it mustn't be that unusual for them to get that kind of order from a secret admirer, Darlene," Dad said. "Just relax. I'm sure there's no real cause for concern."

Was he ever wrong.

CHAPTER FOUR

I felt uneasy when I got to school the next morning. The idea that whoever had sent me the plant was probably right there in the building — maybe sitting at a desk near me in some class or other ... or standing behind me in line at the cafeteria ... or passing me in the hall — really made me nervous.

Discovering that I had a secret admirer might even have been a little flattering if it hadn't been for the message on the card. "*You will always be mine.*" Every time I thought about it, my stomach got a nervous, queasy feeling.

I alternated between wishing this guy would declare himself and hoping he *never* worked up the nerve to say anything. Every time a guy spoke to me or glanced my way I got wondering: could it be him?

One thing is certain: you never know what's going

on inside someone else. A person can look and act perfectly normal, but can be hiding a terrible secret. I've learned that because of some of the things I've been through in the last year or two. It's hard to believe that it was only a little over a year ago that I made up my mind to figure out who was setting the rash of fires that had started springing up here in Little River. Since then, it seems that every time something strange happens, I end up right in the middle of it.

Greg thinks I look for trouble, but that's not exactly true. And he wouldn't mind me getting involved in local mysteries anyway, if it wasn't for the fact that sometimes it can be dangerous.

But this wasn't a mystery, except in the sense that I didn't know who'd sent the plant, and that in itself wasn't exactly ominous.

In any case, the day went by normally, no one came up and blurted out anything about their undying love or anything, and by the time the final bell rang I was starting to relax about the whole thing.

I'd just closed and locked my locker when Greg appeared at my side and announced casually that he was going to walk me home.

"Walk me home?" I echoed. "But why?" He'd never done that before. For one thing, we live in opposite directions. For another, he normally takes a bus, since his place is a couple of kilometres from the school.

"I just feel like it," he said, hoisting my book bag onto his free shoulder.

"Because someone sent me a plant? You have to be kidding!"

"Yeah, well, we don't know who this guy is yet, so I thought it was a good idea to be on the safe side."

"This is ridiculous," I said. I rolled my eyes, too, but I was secretly pleased. "And you're missing your bus."

"It's not like I haven't walked home from your place before," he pointed out.

It was true that we'd walked to each other's places lots of times, except this was different. It seemed like a long walk for him to make for nothing.

I didn't argue, though, since his mind was clearly made up. Anyway, I was glad to be able to spend some extra time with him.

As we walked, I told him about the drama club, and Ms. Lubowski agreeing to let the group perform at least one comedy instead of the old classics she'd picked out.

"So, what did she say when you suggested *The Americans are Coming?*" he asked.

"Not much," I admitted. "She just said she'd think about it. And she said something about getting permission from the author, Herb Curtis, and about adapting it to make it suitable for a school production."

"It sounds like she's interested, anyway," he said.

"I guess." I realized then that Greg was looking around as we walked. It had taken me a few minutes to notice it because he was hardly moving his head at all, but his eyes were moving the whole time, searching ahead and to the sides of us.

"So, you see anything suspicious?" I asked.

He smiled. "Not much gets past you, does it? And no, I haven't noticed anyone around. Not yet, anyway."

A thought hit me. "So, what if this person doesn't tell me who he is for weeks, or even months? What if he never does? Are you going to walk me home every day for the rest of the year?"

"To make sure you're okay? If I need to, I will."

"Well, that's really sweet, but I think you're making way too much of this. I mean, it was just a plant."

"Right. And if the message on the card hadn't been so, well, weird, or if the guy had signed his name, it would be different. The thing is, you don't know who you're dealing with or what might be going on in his head."

"But this is Little River!" I said, half pleased and half exasperated. "It's not like we have a whole lot of psychos running around town."

"Psychos, as you call them," he said with an eyebrow raised, "can be found anywhere. Little River is no exception."

I blushed a little. Greg's dad is a Doctor of Psychology and I knew Greg had been brought up with a respectful attitude toward people with psychological problems. They'd *never* be referred to as psychos in the Taylor house.

"Sorry," I mumbled. Then I changed the subject to the selection we were reading for the book club. The group had decided to read both old and new works, and had chosen an interesting variety, including one book I'd suggested.

It was called *Seventeen* by Booth Tarkington and I'd read it earlier this year, after it had been recommended to me by Ernie's previous owner, Mr. Stanley. It was great, but nearly a hundred years old, so I hadn't really expected anyone else in the room to be familiar with it.

And so, when I'd mentioned the book to the club, it had surprised me to see Webster jump up and shout, "Yes!" and then rave about it with so much enthusiasm that the whole group agreed to put it on our list.

I was curious to know what Greg thought of it. I asked him whether he'd finished it.

"Not yet," he said. "It's really good, though. I just haven't had much time for reading, with all the homework they're piling on this year."

"Tell me about it," I said. "I have so much homework in history and biology that I'll never get through it again before we meet this weekend. It's just lucky for me that I already read *Seventeen* ... though I *do* want to read it at least one more time. It's *so* funny!"

"Is it ever," Greg agreed. "And it really shows what society was like back then — the racial attitudes and the kinds of stereotyping that went on. Some of it's shocking, but it kind of helps you to see prejudice for what it is: pure ignorance and stupidity.

"And the characters!" he continued. He was warming up and I could tell by his tone that he was enjoying the book as much as I had. "I swear, even though the story takes place back in the early 1900s, I know people who are just like some of the characters."

For the rest of the walk to my house, we chatted and laughed about poor Willie Baxter and his increasingly bizarre behaviours, all brought about because of his wild infatuation with Miss Pratt.

Mom was in the kitchen chopping tomatoes when we got to my place. Small bowls were near the cutting board, filled with diced onion and green pepper, shredded cheese and lettuce, and salsa sauce. The smell of taco seasoning, simmering in hamburger in a frying pan on the stove, filled the air.

She looked up in surprise to see Greg with me, and I could tell by the look on her face that she was trying to remember if I'd mentioned anything about bringing him over for dinner.

"Greg walked me home from school," I explained. "He's just going to get a glass of water before he goes home."

"Did something happen? I mean, did anyone bother you today?"

"No, Mom. Nothing like that."

"I'm just being overly cautious," Greg said lightly. I knew his tone was deliberate. He knows what a worrier Mom can be.

"Well, did you find out who sent *that plant*?" she asked. The way she said it, you'd have thought the plant itself was vile and disgusting.

"Not yet."

"Well, I sure appreciate you seeing Shelby home, Greg," Mom said. "Why don't you stay and have a bite to eat with us? If your dad isn't expecting you, that is."

"Actually, he's involved with that research focus group in Viander these days, so he gets home pretty late most evenings," Greg said. "We do a bunch of cooking on the weekend and make up frozen dinners, since our hours are at odds lately. So, I'd love to join you. Thanks."

We were just settling in at the table a while later when the phone rang.

CHAPTER FIVE

"I'll get it," I said, heading to the kitchen. Behind me I heard Dad tell Greg that I normally only jump for the phone that way if I think it might be him calling.

"Hello?"

Silence. Somehow, it seemed heavy and dark.

"Hello?" I could feel my heartbeat quicken.

"Shelby?" The voice was a thick, rasping whisper.

"Who is this?" The words were automatic, but my throat felt dry and constricted. I realized that I sounded scared.

"Shelby." He drew my name out this time, a long, flat sound that sent a chill through me. Oddly, it struck me that it almost sounded like an echo.

"If this is supposed to be some kind of joke," I said, doing my best to keep my voice from shaking, "it isn't one bit funny."

"Oh, Shelby." There was a strangely sinister amusement in his tone. "Don't you know that you belong to me?"

Fear ran through me — a cold bolt that paralysed my voice. I told myself I should hang up, but I was frozen in place, the phone pressed to my ear.

"I will make you my queen."

"Shelby?" Dad called, and for once I was glad about our family rule about no phone interruptions during dinner; Dad would want to know whom I was talking to and why I was on the phone. I heard muffled voices in the next room, and then the sound of a chair being pushed back. Seconds later, Greg came through the kitchen doorway.

"Is everything okay?" he asked. Still unable to speak, I couldn't answer. But he saw my eyes and he knew something was wrong. He stepped toward me.

"Mine for all time," said the voice on the phone. This came out in a burst and was followed immediately by a click. Within seconds, the dial tone followed.

Greg reached me. He steadied me and took the phone, listening. At the same time, he called to my parents.

"He hung up," I managed.

"Did you recognize the voice?"

"No. He was whispering the whole time."

Greg took me to a chair and, once I was in it, he stood behind me with his hands on my shoulders. By then, Mom and Dad were there. They started asking things at the same time until they realized they were only confusing me. Once everyone calmed down a bit, I was able to get the story out.

I felt ridiculous because tears had started and I couldn't seem to stop sobbing. They were only words. In fact, they were only words over the phone. There were no threatening gestures, and I was in no immediate physical danger, and yet I was as terrified as if this person had just cornered me alone somewhere on a dark night.

My heart eventually went back to beating normally — a relief after the frantic pounding in my chest. Things came back into focus, but even so I still felt oddly suspended.

"Randall, we have to call the police," Mom insisted, sounding as though Dad was arguing when, in fact, he was already looking up the number.

Greg suggested dialling star fifty-seven before calling the police. If you dial star fifty-seven in our area, the phone company puts a trace on the call. They won't give you the number, but they *will* give it to the police. Before we could do this, though, the phone rang again. Everyone stopped and looked at each other. Was it *him* again? But it was a neighbour, Marilyn Hester, calling for Mom. She must have been startled at Mom's tone, which was uncharacteristically abrupt.

The call from Ms. Hester lasted less than ten seconds, and yet it robbed us of our best shot to find out this guy's identity. Putting a trace on the last caller now would only produce Ms. Hester's phone number.

A hopeless, sinking feeling washed over me at this realization. We'd just lost an important opportunity, one that could have ended this thing there and then.

"If he calls again, hang up and have the call traced right away," Dad said. "And I'll call the phone company to arrange for caller ID so that we can see who's calling *before* we answer from now on."

I nodded automatically, feeling as though I was somehow to blame. If only I'd thought of calling star fifty-seven as soon as the guy hung up!

Dad called the police, who arrived a short time later. Mom ushered them into the living room. Force of habit, no doubt. The kitchen would have done just as well — better even, because they'd have had the table surface to write the reports in their flip-pads.

Neither officer was familiar to me, though I'd met some members of the force in the past. They identified themselves to me as officers Holt and Stanton.

Holt was older and male, with a square face. He put me in mind of a bulldog, but when he spoke, it was in a kind and fatherly way.

Office Stanton was female, probably thirty at the most. Her approach was matter-of-fact and professional, which I found a bit cold.

They placed themselves one on either side of me, with

Holt on the couch beside me and Stanton in the easy chair. The first few minutes were small talk, probably to relax me. She spoke first when they were ready to take their report.

"Can you tell us what time you received this phone call, Miss Belgarden?"

"It was about five-thirty, I think."

"And can you recount the conversation, as closely as you remember it?" Holt asked.

I did, feeling almost silly. What he'd said to me wasn't nearly as scary sounding when I was telling it as when it was coming at me through the phone. I couldn't capture the tone of his voice, or explain the way it had almost felt as though his breath was coming through the line.

"So," Officer Stanton responded, "the caller said, 'Shelby, Shelby, you belong to me, I'll make you the queen of my world,' and, 'You're mine for all time.' Is that right?"

I nodded, feeling foolish, feeling I shouldn't have bothered them for something so insignificant.

"And that was it?"

"Yes, ma'am." I don't know why I said "ma'am," except that it seemed I ought to.

"Well, you certainly did the right thing calling us." Holt said. "You have to be *really* careful when it comes to things like this."

I felt relieved immediately. Just knowing he was taking it seriously helped, but I couldn't help thinking Stanton figured I was wasting their time, even though she nodded in agreement.

"You don't have call display on your phone?" she asked, though my mom had already told her that.

"No. But Dad said we're going to get it." The only reason we hadn't gotten the service before now was that you have to plug the phone into an electrical outlet for call display to work, and there were none close enough to where our phone was mounted on the wall. And anyway, call display just hadn't seemed important ... until now.

The police went over the call-trace feature with me and told me to call it *first* if the guy phoned me again, and then to contact them immediately afterward.

"When you dial star fifty-seven, the phone company sends a report to their security department right away, so by the time you reach us, they'll have the information in their logs," Holt explained. "That way, we can get it immediately, in case this person is calling from a pay phone, or a friend's place." I promised to do what they told me, and then they each gave me a business card with their contact information. Both of them stopped to talk to Mom and Dad for a few minutes in the other room before they left.

I felt suddenly exhausted, as though I could sleep for days. Greg had joined me again and was sitting next to me on the couch, his arm around my shoulder. I leaned against him. Neither of us spoke.

"Well, I feel a *little* better knowing that the police are involved now," Mom said from the doorway. "Still, I don't want Shelby walking *anywhere* by herself until they find out who this person is."

"I'll be glad to walk her home after school every day," Greg said.

"That's very kind of you, but we couldn't ask that of you, dear," Mom said. "Most days I can pick her up, and her father can drive her every morning. But on the days I can't get her, I'd sure appreciate knowing you were with her."

Greg repeated that he'd be happy to do it, which made my dad, who'd joined Mom, cross the room and shake his hand.

"Now, Darlene, didn't you promise this young man some supper?"

"Oh, my goodness! Of course!" Mom scurried off to reheat the meat for the tortillas and we all headed back to the dining room.

My appetite was completely gone and even the thought of eating made me nauseous, but I joined them anyway. I hate to admit it, but I was really scared just by the idea of being left alone, even if it *was* just in a room in my own house.

CHAPTER SIX

I slept fitfully that night, waking a few times to troubled dreams that broke apart and drifted away like dissipating clouds. Bits of them flashed briefly, freeze frames of fear, before receding into a haze of confusion.

I guess I should have been grateful they didn't stay with me, except I was left with the disquieting feeling that there may have been a clue there, something buried in my subconscious, that could have pointed to the caller's identity.

I wasn't what you'd call energetic at school the next day and it was difficult to focus, either on my classes or on Betts's chatter at lunchtime.

"So, I have this strategy all worked out to snag Kevin," she said, launching into a typical spiel. "You know Edison is his best friend, and Edison's sister is just a year younger than us and she's in tight with Nora Stark, who's also in the drama club. So, I was thinking, all I have to do ..."

She outlined the plan but, quite honestly, all I heard was blah, blah, blah, Kevin, blah, blah, Kevin, blah, blah, blah. Or something like that.

I did my best to hide the fact that I really wasn't listening by smiling and nodding and saying things like, "that sounds good," or "great idea," whenever she paused. When she's in guy-snagging mode, Betts only stops talking when she wants you to agree with what she's saying, so it was a pretty safe cover. In any case, it seemed to work.

You're probably wondering why we weren't talking about the phone call I'd received the night before. The answer to that is simple: I hadn't told Betts anything about it. I also hadn't told her about the plant.

The thing with Betts is that, while she has tons of good qualities, she's not what you'd call terrific at keeping secrets. Truth is, she's a bit of a gossip. And even though she's my best friend and would never deliberately do anything to betray me, she just can't seem to help herself in this one area. You tell her something and she's going to blab it. It's practically guaranteed.

So, it's a limitation I've learned to live with, not being able to trust her with secrets. And that's okay, because my life isn't exactly overrun with clandestine happenings. Usually. So there's not a lot I'd ever wanted to hide from anyone, least of all Betts.

But *this* was definitely in that category. I couldn't tell Betts about it because if I did, it would be all over the school and then the community. The average time for news like that to spread through Little River seems to be on par with the speed of light.

You might think it would be helpful to have other people know some weirdo was bothering me (which is how I still thought of it at that time) since someone might come forward with helpful information. But I knew from watching cop shows on TV that it doesn't usually work that way.

It was more likely that I'd be swamped with a bunch of false leads, which would only confuse me and waste my time. And on top of that, the caller would almost certainly hear the talk. It didn't take a genius to figure out that he'd be extra careful about covering his tracks from then on, and that would only make it harder to catch him.

So, I'd told my folks and Greg that I wanted it kept absolutely quiet. They'd agreed it was the best course of action, and none of them had even asked me if I planned to tell Betts, my best friend. They all know her, so they assumed I'd tell her nothing.

And that's why she didn't know anything about the caller, which brings me back to lunchtime and her prattle about Kevin.

"So," she wound up, "what do you think? You think I'll have a shot?"

Not having actually heard the details of her plan, I wasn't exactly sure how to respond.

"Of course you do!" I said, taking a wild stab. "Any guy would be happy to go out with you."

"Okay, so you're in?" She looked impatient.

In? In on what? I cast about in my head, frantically trying to dredge up even a single detail about her "plan." No such luck.

"Well, you told it all so fast," I said. "Can you go over the part that I have to do again?"

She did, but I have to say I wasn't much further ahead when she finished. It was a long and convoluted scheme that sounded like a bad script for one of those comedies where everything is in a muddle and all of the characters are confused as they dash all over the place doing increasingly odd things.

"All you have to do," Betts told me, waving her hands about as she filled in the details, "is persuade Ina to let me fill in for her at her cafeteria job for a week or so. That will put me next to Carly, who hangs out with Tina and Cheryl … and Cheryl's brother, Hudson, goes out with Marlee. It's perfect!"

"Uh, exactly how is it supposed to work?" I asked. I actually understood the plan *less* after hearing Betts's explanation.

"You talk Ina into giving me her job — just for a while," Betts said patiently, "which gives me a chance to get friendly with Carly, because they work right beside each other."

"And this accomplishes what?"

"It gets me in with the other two — Tina and Cheryl — which gives me a chance to be around Cheryl's brother Hudson. And presto, that connects me to Hudson's girlfriend Marlee, which leads to Kevin's best friend Edison!"

"I don't think that will work," I said hesitantly, trying to unravel the threads of her idea in my head.

"Why not?"

"Well, it just depends on too many things, and some of them are pretty, uh, farfetched. Besides, it would take a long time." I didn't want to sound so critical, but this was one of the craziest ideas Betts had come up with yet — and that's saying something! It was much more likely to end up embarrassing Betts than anything else.

"Well then, how am I going to get him to notice me?"

"Just be yourself, be friendly, and see what happens."

"That won't work, and even if it did it could take months!" Patience isn't one of Betts's strong points, either.

"This all reminds me; I think that one of the guys in drama has a crush on you. Maybe you shouldn't be so closed off to other possibilities."

"Who?"

"Eric."

"Eric Green?"

I nodded. The question was kind of unnecessary, since that was the only Eric in the drama group.

"He sat beside you the last two meetings, remember?"

"He's not after *me*," she said. "If anything, he's after *you*."

"That's ridiculous." My throat went dry almost instantly and I had to gulp down a drink of water before I could talk again. "What would make you say that?"

"'Cause he asked me if you were still going out with Greg."

"When?"

"I dunno. Two or three weeks ago. If he was sitting beside me, it was just to get close to you."

"Or, maybe he was just making conversation and his question about Greg didn't mean anything." In spite of my words, I found myself picturing him calling me, saying those things. It made me wonder if I was going to start suspecting guys randomly on the flimsiest of evidence. Or no evidence at all.

"Whatever. Anyway, I like Kevin, not Eric."

"Okay, okay." The conversation was starting to irritate me. "I wonder where Greg is. He's usually here by now."

As if he'd heard me, Greg came along just then,

sliding into place beside me and taking a sandwich out at the same time.

"I'm starved," he said, taking a huge bite as if to prove it.

"Shelby was just wondering where you were," Betts said.

"I had to take care of something," he answered vaguely. It almost made me smile, because if there's one thing that's certain to get Betts's interest, it's the idea that anyone is deliberately keeping something from her.

"What?" she asked.

"Oh, nothing much. So, what's going on with you two? Anything new?"

"Not really," Betts sighed. "I was just telling Shelby that I ... hey! Do you know Kevin Montoya?"

"A little." Greg failed to notice that I was sending him "don't go there" signals. "He's in my Advanced Math class. Why?"

Her face lit up right away. "I don't know why I didn't think of this before," she said. She gave him a wide, inno-cent smile. "Uh, Greg, could you do me a little favour?"

"Sure," he said, because Greg doesn't know what a "little favour" can turn out to be with Betts Thompson.

CHAPTER SEVEN

Friday evening came with no more contact from whoever had called me. It was starting to feel as though I'd either imagined or exaggerated the whole thing, but I knew that was a dangerous attitude to take. Probably, it was exactly what he wanted: for me to relax, let down my guard ... start to feel safe.

And, even though *I* wanted to be able to relax and feel secure too, I knew I mustn't be fooled by the temporary lull.

I have to tell you, feeling that I wasn't safe was the worst thing I'd ever experienced. I've actually been in situations before where there was a risk — even a big one — but nothing like this. Those were specific moments, events that happened and were over with — fortunately without any real harm to me.

But this! This surrounded me with prickles of fear

every time the phone rang, or whenever I'd imagine some strange movement out of the corner of my eye. I kept reading things into innocent looks and gestures, wondering, wondering ... always wondering, is *this* the guy? Is *that*?

Worse than the external triggers was what was going on in my head. No matter what I was doing or how busy I tried to stay, the fear broke into my thoughts. Someone was out there: someone with strange ideas and obsessions. Someone who, for no reason I could figure out, had chosen me as his target.

A line from a movie, or maybe it was a TV show, kept coming into my head. It was one of those situations where an abused woman was being followed by her ex, and she told a friend, "No matter how careful a person is, if someone out there *really* wants to get them, they're going to."

I did my best to hide the fact that I was scared, but I know my mom and dad could tell. For one thing, I didn't argue about being driven places or always having someone with me wherever I went. Usually it was Greg, but on Friday night he was scheduled at his job at Broderick's Gas Bar, and Betts and I had already planned to go to a new teen flick.

Dad was going to drive me there and Betts and I would walk home afterward, but before we even pulled out of the driveway, Dad had something for me.

"This is a personal alarm," he explained. "If anyone bothers you, you hit this switch and it will set off a kind of siren sound, plus a flash."

I tried it, and was it ever loud!

"And don't just let the alarm do all the work," he added. "Scream, yell, and run. But don't run blindly. Run toward a house, a store, anywhere that there are people. The last thing an attacker wants is to be caught. Noise and flight will make it too hard for him to get to you without being seen. Chances are very good that he'll turn tail and take off. Just attach it to the zipper catch on your jacket."

"Thanks, Dad." I felt close to tears as it hit me that my dad, who'd always been the strongest, most powerful guy in the world to me, was scared. For me.

Then I felt really angry, thinking, what right does this cretin have to come along and upset my life and my parents' lives this way? We're supposed to be safe, living in a small town where everyone knows everyone else.

Of course, they don't really. A town would have to be awfully small for you to know absolutely everyone. But it's still the kind of community where you get the feeling that you're safe, if you know what I mean. Like we're all part of this place and no one is going to go around hurting anyone else.

I shoved aside the fear and anger as best I could when I got to the theatre. Betts was already there, peering out through the large glass window that gives you a clear view of the whole lobby. I told myself I was going to have a good time with my friend and not let any of this bother me.

"Thanks for the drive, Dad, and for the alarm," I said. "We'll be home right after the show."

"If you go anywhere else, be sure to call," Dad said. I promised I would and slid out of the car, waving back to Betts, whose hand was fluttering wildly, like it was even possible that I might not see her in her bright green jacket with a fluffy white collar.

"I got our tickets already," she said, hurrying over and grabbing my arm. "I didn't know what you'd want from concessions, though. Why don't we each get in a line-up and then whoever gets to the counter first can order?"

"What's the big rush? The show doesn't start for another fifteen minutes."

"I want to get a seat in the back row."

"The *back* row?" I was instantly suspicious. Betts is terrified of heights, and even gets dizzy with theatre seating. "You never sit way up there. You can hardly make it halfway."

"Well, I want to this time." She leaned forward and whispered, "I saw Nicki Wooten going in a few minutes ago."

Nicki goes out with Edison, and any time we've seen them at the theatre, they're always in the top row. Of course, in Betts's feverish mind, Edison being there

51

meant there was a chance Kevin would be too, so a seat at the back could mean she'd be near him.

What she apparently hadn't stopped to think through was the fact that if Kevin were there, it would be with a date. He was hardly going to hang out with Edison and Nicki unless they were doubling. I mentioned this to Betts.

"You're right." She sighed and looked so crestfallen that I was almost sorry I'd said anything.

"Come on," I said. "Let's just forget about guys for the evening and enjoy the show."

Easier said than done, considering that the story was one of those light, romantic comedies with a little heartbreak thrown in. On the plus side, there was no sign of Kevin, though there were a lot of guys there who were in the drama club. Besides Edison, we saw Ben Hebert, Jimmy Farrell, Darren Fischer, Tyrone Breau, and their dates all pass us on the way to seats higher up.

From the drama club, Kevin Montoya, Eric Green, and Jimmy Roth were the only three guys who weren't there. Of course, there were lots of other kids we knew at the show that night, too. There's always a crowd the first night of any new teen movie.

It occurred to me that I was paying *particular* attention to who was there from the drama club, and I couldn't help but wonder why. Then, Betts's comments about Eric Green came back to me. That has to be it, I told myself.

I shook these thoughts off and concentrated on the movie, which was kind of fun, but just as predictable as you'd expect. I wonder sometimes why producers even bother with the big dramatic misunderstandings that are supposed to trick you into thinking there's a chance the romance won't work out.

I noticed, when we filed out afterward, that most of the couples seemed a lot cosier than they had been when they arrived. Holding hands, walking closer, smiling at each other. It was like the movie had spread a little dusting of romance over them.

And over Betts, too, judging by her dreamy-eyed comments about how magical it really is when two people are *meant* to be together.

As we walked toward my place, Betts switched topics to lament the loss of The Scream Machine. It used to be the best place in Little River for teens to hang out, a place where they served greasy food and thick milkshakes and didn't care if you were a bit noisy. But it was sold earlier this year, and the new owner changed the name to "River Belle" and turned it into one of those fancy dessert places with specialty coffee. The booths were gone, replaced by tiny round tables and wrought iron chairs. None of us felt comfortable there anymore, but even if we had, the crazy prices would have driven us away.

As occupied as we were talking about this injustice, it would have been easy not to see him. Really, it's a wonder that I noticed him at all.

It was the way he was moving that drew my attention. He was across the street and a few yards behind us. My peripheral vision caught him as we turned onto my street.

Beside me, Betts was still talking, but I no longer heard her. I fought down the panic that told me to grab her arm and run like mad for my place.

There's no danger, I told myself. I'm not alone and I have my alarm with me. Everyone on this street knows me. Help is right here.

"This is my chance." I told myself that if I could just get a look at his face, at least I'd know whom I was dealing with.

"What?" Betts bent her head to one side, her face curious.

I realized I'd spoken aloud, even if it was in a hushed voice. I held a finger up to signal "just a second" to Betts, and tried to look casual as I bent down and fiddled with my shoelace. As I did, I watched him move another step or two. Then he paused. I could read uncertainty in his body language as he tried to decide whether or not I'd noticed him.

The unfortunate thing — and for sure it was deliberate — was that he was wearing a big sweatshirt with the hood up. There was no way to see his face from where Betts and I were stopped.

I willed him to come a bit closer, to get right underneath the streetlight that was just yards away from him, but he wasn't budging. In fact, he started to edge backward without taking any actual steps.

When I stood back upright, it was like I'd given him a signal. He turned and ran, racing along the street, past a few houses, and then disappearing behind a hedge that lined someone's driveway. Assuming he'd gone through their backyard, he'd be a block over and near an intersection that would give him four directions from which to choose his next move.

"Who was that?"

I knew I had no choice then. Betts was staying for the night and I was going to have to tell my parents about this as soon as I got home. I took a deep breath, swore her to secrecy about five times, and then told her what was going on.

She was the first one to use the word I'd been refusing to accept, probably because it just made the whole thing seem worse.

"A stalker!"

CHAPTER EIGHT

"**Y**ou have no idea who it was?"

I was tired of the question, which Betts had asked at least four times since we'd reached my place. Now, I don't like to be suspicious of her motives, since she *is* my best friend and all. I kept thinking that of *course* she wouldn't be enjoying any of this, but she did sound almost, well, *excited* about the whole thing.

My parents had, as you might expect, been very upset to hear about the guy who was following us. They called the police right away and then we all sat and waited for them.

The officers who came were new to me and I ended up explaining the whole thing from the start, even though they'd been briefed at work on my original complaint.

This pair, both male, seemed terribly mismatched personality-wise, and I couldn't help but wonder how they managed to work together. One, Officer Nash, had a friendly, relaxed approach, but the other, Officer Mueller, was stone-faced and abrupt. He made me feel as though I were making the whole thing up. And, unfortunately, he did most of the talking.

"So, Miss Belgarden, what makes you think this person was following you?" Mueller asked after I'd gone over what had happened.

"Well, he had his face hidden, you know, with the hood, and when he realized that I'd noticed him, he took off running the other way."

"Maybe he had his hood up because he was cold," Mueller said.

I didn't know how to argue with that.

"If you didn't see this person's face, how can you be sure it was a male?"

"Well, the way he walked, and his build. And the way he ran when he took off."

"Uh huh. And you're quite certain he ran because you looked at him and not because he'd suddenly remembered he was late for something, or because he realized he was on the wrong street?"

"If you don't mean to take this seriously," my father's voice cut in from the doorway behind me, "please let me know right now so that I can ask to have someone else sent out. My daughter is *not* the hysterical type and she is *not* imagining this. This person has already contacted Shelby twice. His messages have been disturbing and bordering on threatening."

"Sir, with respect to tonight's incident," Mueller said, seemingly unruffled by my dad's words. "I am simply trying to determine whether or not there is enough evidence for us to act on the complaint. I don't doubt that someone has bothered your daughter. I'm just questioning whether or not this pedestrian is related to the earlier incidents. We can't chase after everyone who happens to be walking down the street near your daughter."

My dad took a couple of steps toward him, his eyes blazing, but before he could speak, Officer Nash broke in.

"Of course, Officer Mueller doesn't mean to imply that we don't plan to take Shelby's complaint seriously," he said. "We have her description and we'll cruise around and look for this person, though chances are he's disappeared by now. And we'll see that your house is patrolled throughout the night. In the meantime, if you see or hear anything suspicious, and I mean *anything*, you be sure to call us right away."

Mueller looked kind of annoyed and I realized with a start that he'd actually been hoping for a confrontation. Not a good sign in a cop, if you want my opinion. He put me more in mind of a school bully than someone who was supposed to serve and protect.

Dad, on the other hand, is pretty even-tempered. It takes a lot to get him angry, but Mueller had done it without trying. Even so, he calmed down quickly when Nash assured him they were going to follow up on what I'd told them.

I wondered, if it had just been Mueller, what he'd have done. As it stood, I had a pretty good feeling that Nash would see to it that they did a thorough check of the neighbourhood. I did agree with him, though, that it was unlikely they'd find anyone.

The main thing I'd been able to tell them was that the guy had the hood of his sweatshirt pulled up. It would be easy enough for him to take it down and tuck it inside. Then he could walk around as casual as you please without so much as drawing a glance from anyone.

If only I'd been able to see his face. Just one glimpse could have ended this thing right there. It could also have ended Betts's annoying repetitions that I must have *some* idea who it was, followed by questions asking who did I *think* it was, and what could this guy *want*, and on and on.

"Betts, honestly, I have no idea. Not a clue."

"Yeah, but do you think it's someone from school?"

"Probably, but I don't know for sure."

"Well, he must know you from somewhere," she pressed, determined to pin me down on at least one point.

"I guess."

"So, if he's not from school, where do you … hey! Maybe it's that guy who works at The Korner Store!"

"Betts ..."

"You know — the one with the crooked smile! That would be cool. He's *cute*!"

"Don't be ridiculous. It's not The Korner Store guy, and anyway, who *cares* if the stalker is cute or not?" I asked, exasperated. "He's turning my life into a nightmare. The phone rings and I jump. Every time I walk down the street I wonder if he's watching me. This isn't some kind of game, Betts. It's real. And it's *scaring* me."

She finally seemed to get it. At least, she stopped talking about it like it was a romantic movie or something, and started taking it seriously.

We went around a few different ideas, and I made notes. I've always found it helps to write things down, but there hardly seemed to be any point in writing this stuff. None of it was likely to point to the culprit. I did it anyway, probably from force of habit, and this is what I ended up with:

1) *Plant.* White calla lily. Delivered around five p.m. on November 27th. Note said, "You will always be mine." Delivery had been arranged by mail by a person unknown.

2) *Phone call.* Said things like he was going to make me his queen and that I belong to him and I was his for all time. Spoke in a creepy whisper.

3) *Followed me home from theatre.* Person wore

jeans and dark blue sweatshirt with hood pulled up. Average build. Probably between 5' 9" and 6' tall. Ran off when spotted.

"Well," Betts said when I'd finished, "at least you know you'll have other chances, unless he decides to just give up."

Other chances. I knew she meant to cheer me, but her words had the opposite effect. The worst thing was, she was right. I didn't know much about stalkers, but I did know this: they hardly ever give up.

I'd almost certainly hear from this guy again. The question was, would I *see* him too, and if I did, would I be in danger?

CHAPTER NINE

The next morning I felt about as rested as if I'd spent the night doing aerobics. A shower helped a little, but I was still somewhat groggy when I made my way to the kitchen. Maybe breakfast would help.

Mom and Dad were at the table, coffee cups in front of them. They both looked as tired as I felt.

"Hey, sunshine," Dad said. "You sleep okay?" His voice sounded cheerful and he smiled, but the smile stopped before it got to his eyes.

"I guess. Any sign of Betts?" I glanced around, as if they might be hiding her in the cupboards or something.

"Not yet," Mom said. "But she's not really an early riser, as I recall."

"True." I smiled at the thought of how grumpy Betts can be if you wake her before ten o'clock (at the earliest) on a Saturday. She'll make these weird, growling noises that sound like there's a bear in the bed, and cling to her blanket as if it's the most valuable thing in the whole world. Honestly, I don't know how she manages to get up for school through the week.

"I caught Ernie trying to sneak into her room this morning," Mom told me. "She hadn't shut the spare room door tightly and he was pushing it open with his head when I spotted him."

"Could have been the end of him," Dad said.

"Yeah, she probably wouldn't have given him the warmest possible welcome," I agreed. Ernie isn't exactly subtle when he wants to wake someone up. I couldn't picture Betts taking kindly to his cold nose, tickly whiskers, and rough tongue on her face — and that's just when he's getting started.

"Speaking of Ernie, Mr. Stanley is visiting today," Mom said.

I'd completely forgotten that this was one of the weekends when Mr. Stanley spends part of the day with our family. He comes every second week, usually right after lunch, and stays through dinner, returning to his nursing home around seven or eight in the evening.

He isn't a relative or anything, and we've only known Mr. Stanley for a few months, so it might seem strange that we have him over so often if you don't know that he's Ernie's original owner. I first met him a while back when I was trying frantically to find out what had happened to a co-worker who'd disappeared. Our paths crossed again later on when I was passing his apartment building and I saw him on a stretcher being taken to an ambulance. I offered to babysit Ernie while he was in the hospital, an arrangement that became permanent when he moved into a nursing home.

"We're having Malcolm and Greg for dinner tonight as well," Mom added as she went to the counter and brought over the coffee pot to refill her cup.

This was news to me, but I was more than happy to hear it. Greg and I hadn't talked about plans for the evening, though it was understood we'd be getting together. With so few things for teens to do in Little River, we often just walked around, rented movies, browsed through the stores at the mall, or hung out with friends.

Late fall and winter are the worst months for us. We're both big on nature and in the summer we spend a lot of time exploring through the woods and along the river. We've even found a few secret spots that you could walk right by and not see if you don't know they're there.

But there isn't much to do there this time of year. A lot of the animals disappear for the winter. Beavers and muskrats go into their dens while skunks, raccoons, and bears spend the season hibernating. Deer and moose disappear into the deeper woods, so the chance of spotting any wildlife at the year's end isn't great.

Those that *are* still around aren't usually easy to spot. Mostly, they're predators like mink, otter, bobcat, and fox. Of course, there are always rabbits around, but they're fast and cautious and we rarely see them at any time of year.

It's not just the lack of wildlife that makes the woods less appealing at the end of November. By then, the deciduous trees are bare, the wildflowers are gone, and the whole place feels kind of deserted. Sometimes it's even spooky.

Anyway, with so little to do around here, especially in the cold months, it was kind of nice to have plans with our parents. Of course, Greg and I could just hang out and listen to music or rent a movie or whatever after dinner, but this gave us another option. If we wanted to, we could talk our parents into playing a game with us.

Picking a game can take a while. Mom always tries to talk us into Scattergories (which Dad hates because he gets confused and uses the wrong letters) or Balderdash, while Dr. Taylor likes Mad Gab even though, quite frankly, he's terrible at it.

Before I got any further with these thoughts, Betts appeared in the kitchen. She said good morning to all of us, slid into the empty chair at the table, and looked around hopefully.

"Betts, honey, what would you like for breakfast?" Mom asked at once. Betts always makes a big deal of Mom's cooking, which gets her special treatment whenever she's over at mealtime.

"I wouldn't want you to go to any trouble," Betts lied.

"Don't be silly, dear. It's no trouble at all."

"Well, if you're sure…. I was just thinking of the awesome omelette you made the last time I stayed over. If it's honestly not a bother."

By the time she'd said "bother," Mom was already at the fridge getting out the eggs and other ingredients. She makes these fantastic spicy omelettes with tomatoes and cheese and cayenne pepper and whatever else strikes her as a good idea to toss in at the time.

"Did you want one too, Shelby?"

"I think I'll just have cereal," I said. "Thanks, though."

"You forgot to ask me," Dad said.

"I didn't forget, Randall," Mom told him sternly. "You had eggs a few days ago, and you know you're supposed to be watching your cholesterol. Besides, you already had your breakfast."

"If you can call that breakfast," Dad sulked. (He'd just finished yogurt, a banana, and a slice of toast with apricot preserves.) "I must say, this is a fine way to treat a man in his own house."

"Yeah, that's too bad," Betts said without the slightest trace of sympathy.

Dad sighed and looked mournful. Mom told him to

stop putting on the dog, whatever that means, and he gave up, finished his coffee, and went off to the other room.

I poured a bowl of Apple Cinnamon Cheerios and munched on them while Betts ate her omelette. As she chewed, she made a lot of enthusiastic "Mmm" sounds so it was probably just as well that Dad wasn't there.

After we finished eating we helped Mom with the dishes. Betts had plans to go shopping with her cousin after lunch, so she headed home not long afterward. I did my chores, worked on some homework, and grated some carrots for a cake Mom was making.

Dad went and fetched Mr. Stanley just after one o'clock. I met them at the back door, hugged Mr. Stanley, and took him into the living room where he settled into Dad's favourite chair. Mom or I would get chased out, but Dad lets Mr. Stanley sit there every week.

"I don't suppose the little rascal is around," our guest said as soon as he was comfortable.

"Ernie!" I couldn't believe I hadn't thought to round him up, like I do every time Mr. Stanley is coming. "I'll go find him right now."

I hunted through the house calling his name, but there was no sign of him. He was either hiding or outside.

"I might have let him out earlier," Mom said when I asked if she'd seen him.

Great! If he'd gone wandering around the community it might take hours to find him, and I knew how important spending time with Ernie was to Mr. Stanley.

"I think he might be outside," I reported, before I threw on my jacket and went to look. "I'm sure it will just take a minute to find him."

"You're a good girl," Mr. Stanley said. He tells me that almost every time I see him.

I searched the yard quickly and then, when he didn't appear, started down the street, calling his name and telling him he had a special visitor. Mr. Stanley once told me that Ernie could understand what you were saying to him and even though I doubted it, there seemed no harm in trying.

I'd made two passes up and down our street and was almost right in front of my house again when I heard Ernie kind of yowl, which is his peculiar way of letting you know he is displeased with something.

"Ernie?" The sound seemed to have come from a hedge along the back of our yard.

Sure enough, when I got near the hedge, he suddenly burst out, streaking across the yard to the back step and pacing frantically until I crossed the yard and opened the door for him.

I scooped him up and carried him through to the other room, where his former owner sat, anxiously waiting to see him. The second we came into view, Mr. Stanley's eyes lit up and his face was kind of transformed. It was almost like he looked younger.

"He was hiding," I reported, passing Ernie to him. "Out in the hedge. I found him after I wasted a good fifteen minutes looking up and down the street."

"By yourself?" Dad looked at me with alarm.

"Oh." I'd forgotten all about not going anywhere alone. "Sorry. Anyway, it was okay. No one was around."

"Now, what have you been into?" Mr. Stanley asked Ernie as he snuggled him, his face pressed against Ernie's head. "You smell kind of funny."

"Goodness knows what he's been up to out there," I said. "Does he smell like a cedar hedge?"

"No, it's more … I don't know, exactly. Perfume maybe."

I leaned over and sniffed Ernie, who responded by purring loudly and rubbing his face against my nose. He did have a scent clinging to him, but I didn't know what it was.

"Who knows what he got into," I said, giving him a little cheek rub. "Anyway, he's sure glad to see you."

"I'm glad to see him, too," Mr. Stanley said fondly. Then, chuckling a little with embarrassment, he added that he was also glad to see the rest of us.

The remainder of his visit passed uneventfully, with Ernie sticking around and behaving reasonably well. Mr. Stanley seemed to enjoy meeting Greg and Dr. Taylor, and I could tell they took to him too. As for me, I was just happy there'd been no sign of the stalker.

CHAPTER TEN

"What you *need*," Webster was saying, "is a *passion* for your work. If the reader is to *feel* the words you must first *live* them, *breathe* them, *become* them."

I wasn't sure how you'd go about "becoming" words, but I kept myself from asking. Lately, it seemed if you asked Webster a question about something he'd said, he took it as a challenge of some sort and launched into a lengthy, defensive spiel that didn't actually give you an answer.

The others must have caught on as well, because no one ever had questions for him anymore, though there'd been lots the first couple of months we'd been meeting. Back then he'd listen thoughtfully and give answers that made sense. The last few meetings, though, he'd seemed unfocused and, well, kind of *off*, if you know what I mean. He'd rave, and what he'd say wouldn't make a whole lot of sense. And it was usually unconnected to whatever we were talking about at the time.

On this day, we sat quietly and waited for him to finish talking, which was the way we'd become accustomed to responding lately. Sitting next to me, Greg ventured a glance in my direction and I saw his eyebrows go up slightly, but he was as silent as everyone else.

Mr. Grimes was the one who broke in, offering a weak comment about how he was sure that what Webster was saying was very helpful, but perhaps we should get back to the book.

"You'd like that, wouldn't you?" Webster said. It was an odd thing to say, but even more peculiar than that was the fact that he never opened his mouth again for the rest of the evening. He just sat, looking around from person to person with a strangely intense look on his face.

It was really starting to freak me out and when I felt his gaze on me I tried hard not to look back. It was impossible. As though drawn magnetically, I found my head tilting up and my eyes meeting his.

A smile twitched at one corner of his mouth. It was gone so fast that I wondered later if I might have imagined it. Seconds later his look shifted, moving on to someone else.

He's lost his mind, I thought. Or maybe he's on something. But of course, I didn't voice either of those opinions out loud. Like the rest of the group, I did my best to act as if everything was perfectly normal.

You ever notice how hard that is to do? The more you try to act natural, the more obvious it is that you're acting. It's like every word and gesture is overdone. Smiles are exaggerated, anything you say comes out sounding not-quite-right, and you feel like your face is frozen with an expression that doesn't quite fit.

It was like torture trying to get through the rest of the meeting. I can't remember a thing that was said, only that we were all doing our best to pretend we didn't notice Webster sitting there looking from person to person, around the circle, again and again.

When it finally ended we all left in a hurry, like they might lock the doors if we didn't get out quickly enough. Once outside we stood huddled in a silent cluster, as if obeying some unspoken command, until we saw Webster exit the side door, get into his car, and drive off.

As soon as he was gone, nervous laughter and talk started up. It seemed we all needed to make sure everyone else had felt the same thing at the meeting.

"I'm telling you, he's gone psycho," Bruce Kerr said, tapping a finger against the side of his head.

"I don't even want to stay in the book club if he's going to be there," Sheri Poitras said. This drew murmurs of assent from Holly Holmes and Nora Stark.

"He's getting spooky, all right. And did you see the weird look he gave Shelby?" Jason Puckett said, confirming what I'd noticed earlier. "He has no right to do that."

Greg suggested we discuss it with Mr. Grimes. "We're going to have to tell him we're not comfortable with Webster there," he said.

"But Webster comes as a courtesy — to help us," Sharon Marsh objected. "It would be insulting to tell him not to come anymore."

"So, we're supposed to put up with whatever craziness he wants to dish out?" Jimmy Roth asked. "If we don't want him around, we shouldn't have to put up with him."

"Yeah, but he's a published author," Sharon said. It was an empty argument and made no sense, but Sharon is one of those super-nice people who never want to hurt anyone's feelings. I knew she was just as uncomfortable with Webster around as the rest of us were, but she couldn't bear the thought of making him feel bad.

After a few more minutes it was decided that Jimmy and Sheri would go in and take the group's message to Grimes. The rest of us waited outside.

They were back in no time, walking fast and looking guilty. Jimmy gave us the news.

"We didn't get to talk to him," he explained. "When we got to the classroom he was on his cell phone …"

"Talking to someone about Webster!" Sheri cut in. "He was telling whoever it was that Webster seems to be having some kind of psychotic breakdown. Then he said something about contacting his family to see if he's taking his medication."

"And he said Webster has a history of not taking his pills when he's writing because he thinks they interfere with his muse or something." Jimmy rolled his eyes.

"We didn't know what to do. I mean, we couldn't barge in while he was on the phone. Grimes would have known we'd heard what he was saying," Sheri said.

"A psychotic breakdown," Greg said.

"Hey, your dad's a shrink, right?" Lynn Wilcox smiled at Greg. I've noticed that she smiles at him a lot. "He'd probably know what kind of mental problem would make Webster act that way. Maybe you could ask him."

"Or maybe we could cut Webster a little slack for the time being," Greg said. "It sounds like Mr. Grimes knows something needs to be done about this. Let's just leave it at that and see what he does. We'll be able to tell if the problem is fixed the next time Webster comes to a meeting."

"Yeah, I think Greg's right," Nora said. "I mean, if the guy has problems ..."

"That's right! The least we can do is be under-standing," Sharon said. She looked really relieved.

EYES OF A STALKER

The whole group agreed with Greg's suggestion. Even Annie Berkley spoke up, and she's the quietest member of the group. Most of us know little about her other than her name and the fact that she lives in a foster home. I was surprised that she even joined the book club. Annie reads a lot — she often has a book with her even at lunchtime — but she's also really shy.

Once it was decided that we'd wait and see what happened with Webster, the group broke up, heading off in different directions. A few kids got picked up, but most of us walked.

I was glad to have Greg with me and I noticed once again that he was keeping close watch on both sides of the street as we walked along.

"I think maybe whoever it is has given up," I said. "There's been no sign of him since last Friday … and I'm actually starting to doubt myself about that. Maybe I just imagined that guy was following me. Or maybe whoever it was didn't know I already had a boyfriend and then he found out I do so he's backing off. There's been nothing for almost a week. Maybe it's over."

"That's a lot of 'maybes,'" Greg said. "And a week isn't very long. I hope you're not letting your guard down."

"Of course not. I'll be careful until I'm sure. But whoever it was probably realized he was being ridiculous and stopped."

We were close to my place by then, and in spite of the confidence I'd put into my voice just a moment before, I jumped and gasped when a car suddenly pulled up beside us with a blast from the horn.

"It's just your dad," Greg said. "Looks like he's going to give me a drive home."

I laughed at my own cowardice and we got into the car. Even so, it took almost all the way to Greg's place and back for my heart to stop beating faster than normal.

Feeling a little silly, I had a snack and then went to my room and booted my computer. I had an essay to finish by the end of the week, and it wasn't going so well. That's one kind of writing assignment I don't particularly like, so I wanted to get it out of the way as soon as possible.

Of course, I *had* to check my e-mail before I actually started working. And when I did, what I saw there sent a chill of horror right through me.

CHAPTER ELEVEN

The sender's name was a typical kind — a nickname (soreros) with a bunch of numbers behind it. It meant nothing to me. I just figured it was either junk mail or someone from school whose e-mail address was unfamiliar to me ... until I clicked on it and started reading.

I stared at the words on the screen. I read them again and again. It was as if shock had immobilized me and I was frozen there, forced to go over and over the ugly message. A message that reached right into my house — right into my room.

So you think I have given up? As if I would give up what is rightfully mine. As if you can just walk away, when you are my destiny. It seems that you do not yet understand that YOU BELONG TO ME.

Words spoken must be paid for. We will see who is RIDICULOUS!!!!! Perhaps your so-called boyfriend will not be so appealing when I am done.

But YOU — you will be given a second chance. If you are wise, you will not anger me again.

There was a strange, distant sound echoing in my head, like water crashing on the beach.

"He heard me," I whispered to my empty room. "He heard me talking to Greg."

Woodenly, I stood and made my way down the hall. I found Mom and Dad in the kitchen drinking tea and playing chess. My eyes went to the board automatically, but the pieces swam into a blur.

"Shelby!" Mom cried. She was already standing, reaching for me. "What is it?"

"An e-mail." It was all I could get out before something cracked in me. I found myself crying. I kept trying not to. I told myself it was silly and wasn't going to help anything, but the tears wouldn't stop.

Mom held me while Dad went to my room and read the message. I heard the printer whirring and seconds later he came back down the hall.

"It looks like this creep has just made the mistake that will lead us to him," he said as he walked to the phone. "They'll be able to find out who he is by tracing this message."

"But it's just a Yahoo account," I said. "There's no way he'd have put his real information in when he created it."

"Doesn't matter. They can find out *where* a message was sent from," Dad said.

I hadn't known that, and I wondered if the police would. When the squad car arrived in response to Dad's call, I was dismayed to see Officer Mueller come through the door alone. He looked over the message Dad had printed out and then turned to me.

"Do you know what this means?" He pointed to the line that said, "*We will see who is RIDICULOUS!!!!!*"

"It looks like he was somewhere nearby when I was talking to my boyfriend a while ago." I explained the conversation we'd had, and how I'd made a comment that maybe whoever was bothering me had realized it was ridiculous and had given up.

Mueller stood silently for a couple of seconds when I'd finished talking. Then he turned to my dad.

"Mr. Belgarden, I'm going to post a car in front of your house tonight. Tomorrow, we'll see if we can trace the source of this message. However, even if we're able to locate and charge this person, we may not be able to hold him for any length of time. How soon he'd be back on the street would depend on the charge, and whether or not the judge remanded him or let him out pending trial. I'd like to suggest that you get a home alarm company in to install a good security system. Something that covers every possible entrance."

"It'll be done first thing in the morning," Dad said. He looked as surprised as I felt, and I knew he hadn't expected Mueller to take the e-mail as seriously as he had.

Mueller went over some basic precautions. Some I was already doing, like not walking anywhere by myself, but others might never have entered my mind. He said I should stay away from windows and that we should keep the curtains closed after dark in case this weirdo was watching the house.

"Stalkers don't lay low for long. They tend to be driven to send messages and sometimes 'souvenirs' of some description. The meaning of anything he might leave may not be clear to you — you might not even be sure it's from him — but don't dismiss a single thing that shows up and seems out of place. Call us. This guy *wants* you to be thinking about him, so it's almost guaranteed that he'll contact you again soon.

"And," he added, "if Shelby should receive any unexpected mail through postal delivery, please don't open it. Handle it as little as possible and call us."

"How will we know if it's from this, this *person*, or just something innocent?" Mom asked.

"We won't know until it's opened," Mueller said, "but if it *is* from the stalker, we'll have a better chance of getting his prints if no one else has touched it."

He went over the different precautions he'd suggested once more and then told us someone would be over in the morning to look into the e-mail I'd received.

"We'll also send someone over to the Taylor house to let Greg and his father know about the threat, and ask them to be extra cautious," he added. "And we'll have their house patrolled."

When he was getting ready to leave, Dad shook his hand and told him we all appreciated the way he was taking care of things. He didn't add that it was kind of a surprise to us, since Mueller had acted pretty sceptical the last time he was here. It was easy to see that the e-mail had convinced him that this was real. Now that he was on board, he was sure doing everything possible to help.

I kept telling myself that as soon as they sent someone to trace the source of the e-mail, it would be over. We'd know who this creep was, and I figured that, once he was exposed, he'd pretty well have to stop.

On the phone later, Greg and I talked about the e-mail. He agreed that the police should be able to find out where it came from. I told him I was sure that would put an end to the whole thing.

"I hope you're right," he said.

"Well, as long as they can find out who it is ..."

"You think this guy will stop what he's doing as soon as his identity is known?"

"Well, sure. Don't you?"

"I don't know, Shelby. I mean, I don't think stalkers usually give up that easily."

"Maybe not guys who are after someone for a long time," I said. "But this guy just started bothering me. Don't you think he'll quit if he's stopped this fast?"

"It would be great if he did," Greg agreed, "but you have to remember he didn't just start doing this out of the blue. He must have been obsessed with you for a while, and that had to grow enough for him to start acting on it. You're just seeing it now, but I don't think it just started."

"That's encouraging." My voice was angry, and even though I didn't mean it to be directed at Greg, that's how it sounded.

"I'm sorry. I'm not trying to upset you, Shelby. Don't you think *I* want this jerk to leave you alone? Of course I do. But I also want you to be careful. Really careful. You can't let your guard down until you're sure it's safe."

"I know, Greg. I do. It's just that, well, you have no idea what this is like. I feel like someone's watching me all the time. Watching and planning ... something. Only I don't know what. Or when. It's like being hunted or something."

"I'm sorry, hon. I just wish I could do something."

"I know you do. So do I. I think that's the worst part. I feel so *helpless*. I mean, I don't even know who this psychopath *is*, let alone how to handle all of this."

We talked for a while longer, mostly about other things, and it helped a bit. But once we said goodnight it all came back, and I realized this thing had taken over my life. It was in the back of my head all the time, even when I was not consciously thinking about it.

It wasn't just scaring me. It was wearing me down.

I crawled into bed that night and lay there awake in the dark and feeling very alone for a long time. After a while I found myself crying — softly, so I wouldn't disturb my parents.

I kept thinking that it wasn't fair, that I hadn't done anything to deserve what was happening. Of course, that must be true of anyone who's ever been tormented by a stalker. It's just hard to remember sometimes that it's not your fault.

After a few moments, Ernie left his usual place on my spare pillow, crept over, and head-butted me. He plunked down on my pillow and stuck his cold nose on my cheek.

It was oddly comforting having him there. I wiped the tears away and concentrated on the soft sound of his purring.

At last, I fell asleep.

CHAPTER TWELVE

It's funny how differently things look after you've slept and woken to a day where the sun shines and the world looks normal. That's how it was the next morning when Dad drove me to school. It was bright outside, the air was cool and crisp, and it seemed impossible that this nightmare could really be going on in my life.

"Oh! Can you let Mom know that I have a drama club meeting right after school?" I asked Dad as I got out of the car. "It'll probably be over at around 4:30 or 5:00. I'll call when I'm ready."

As usual, Betts was waiting near the front entrance for me. Only this time she wasn't alone. Jimmy Roth was standing by her and they seemed to be deep in conversation. He turned with a smile when I reached them.

"I was just telling Betts about Webster and how freaky he's getting," he said. "We should write our own play about him for drama." He paused to make bug-eyes and twist his mouth in a weird shape. "We could call it 'The Author Who Flipped Out.'"

Betts giggled, soaking up the gossip.

"Yeah, well, last night we all agreed to give him a break," I reminded him, annoyed that he was spreading this around, "so I don't think that's the greatest idea."

"I'm just kidding," he said right away. "You don't have to take everything so seriously."

"Okay, but I still don't think any of us should be discussing him," I said, "especially since we know he has, uh, problems. This kind of talk could ruin his reputation."

"Oh, don't be ridiculous," Jimmy said with a slow smile. "Anyway, writers *want* people to think they're eccentric."

"Whatever," I said, still angry. I told myself I was overreacting because of everything that was going on. "Anyway, I have to go. I need to get some stuff out of my locker before class."

"You *do* go a bit overboard sometimes," Betts said as we made our way down the hall.

"About what?"

"Don't snap at me. Anyway, I mean, you know, about not gossiping. Like, if someone acts all psycho in front of a whole group of kids, you think that's going to stay quiet? In Little River?"

She was right. There was no way there wasn't going to be talk about Webster.

"Yeah, well, I don't have to be part of it," I said.

"No, but you don't have to jump down someone's throat over it either."

"I'm surprised at you," I added, though that was an out-and-out lie. "You've seen how much harm gossip can do."

"This is different," she insisted. "Anyway, maybe we should just drop it."

Typical, I thought. The second Betts thinks she's going to lose an argument, she changes the subject. Then I decided I wasn't being fair.

"I'm just so stressed," I said, and I told her about the e-mail I'd received the night before.

"You mean he was stalking you when Greg was walking you home?"

"There's no other explanation for it."

"That is *so* creepy." Betts shivered and looked around. She lowered her voice to a whisper, even though there were only a few students at the lockers, and none of them seemed to be paying the least attention to us. "Do you think he could be listening to us right now?"

"I doubt it," I said, but I found that I was whispering, too.

"So, you think the police will really find out who it is today? After they check the e-mail and stuff?"

"Hopefully." I thought it was odd how normal my voice sounded, as if it wasn't that big a deal to me. The truth was, it was pretty much all I thought about all day. I somehow managed to get through my classes, but I was really tempted to ditch drama.

"Let me use your cell phone," I said to Betts when we got to our lockers. "I think I'll call Mom to come and get me now. I don't think I can handle drama today."

"I don't blame you," she said as she dug through her book bag. "Now where is that thing? I'm sure I put it in here this morning.... Oh, wait, here it is."

I dialled our number and listened while the phone rang seven times. "No answer," I said. "That's odd. Mom knew she had to pick me up today."

"Did she know you were supposed to have drama?"

"I told Dad to let her know."

"So, she's out because she thinks you won't need a drive for another hour."

"I guess so. It looks like I'm stuck here, then."

"You can probably catch Greg before his bus leaves," Betts suggested.

"No. I mean, I know he'd walk me home if I asked him to, but when I mentioned that I had drama after school today and Mom would be picking me up, he said that was great because he needs to study for a big history test he has coming up."

"So, what ... are you going to stay then?"

"I guess."

"You might be able to get a drive home with someone else," she said.

"No, I'll just go to drama after all, and call Mom later." I didn't want to admit to Betts that I was afraid to be home alone, even for such a short time. To be perfectly honest, it wasn't easy to admit that even to myself.

The drama club meets in the auditorium, which Ms. Lubowski insists on calling the theatre. Almost everyone else was already there when Betts and I arrived and took our seats. I heard Betts sigh and, seeing that the chairs around Kevin were all occupied, I knew I didn't need to ask why. A mean thought flashed through my head that it served her right if she never got to sit next to him, much less go out with him, after dragging me into something I knew I was going to hate.

Of course, I felt ashamed of myself immediately, and I made up my mind that I'd try to be more supportive and helpful. Not that there was a whole lot I could do, but maybe I could try to get there early next time and pick seats near Kevin. He wouldn't think anything of that, since everyone knows I'm going out with Greg.

These thoughts were interrupted by Ms. Lubowski, who had risen and gone to stand in front of us.

"Group, can I have your attention please?" she said. "There has been some discussion about which plays we're going to put on. I have decided that, in the spirit of democracy, we will choose the second and third plays as a group. First, however, we will proceed with *Macbeth*. This will give everyone time to think about what they'd like to do next."

This announcement brought on a buzz of whispers, which was silenced when she lifted her hand. "Today we're going to go over some suggested readings you may select for your tryouts. I'd like each of you to come ready to read for a part at our meeting next week."

A pause, and then, "After all, this is what we've been leading up to the past weeks, with our mini skits and breathing exercises and voice projections and all of the other things we've practised over and over."

Right. All of the things that felt silly and unnatural when we were doing them, I thought.

"I know this is an exciting time for you," she continued, "so I hope no one will be too terribly disappointed if they don't get a part for our very first play."

I know I'll survive, I thought, almost laughing out loud at the idea of being crushed because I didn't get to make a big fool of myself on stage in front of an audience.

"And I want to reassure you ahead of time that everyone will be on stage before the year ends!" Ms. Lubowski clasped her hands together in delight at this reassurance. I figured I could always drop out of the club by the next play anyway if I wanted to. By then, Betts would probably have lost interest in Kevin.

That reminded me that she'd asked Greg to do something for her, only she hadn't said what. I was making a mental note to ask her about it after the meeting (it's always good to know what kind of mess your boyfriend's gotten himself into) when her cell phone rang.

"Oh, sorry," she said, fumbling through her things for it. "I forgot to turn it off."

"It's all right," Ms. Lubowski said. "Just make it quick."

Betts nodded as she said hello.

"What do you mean, who is this?" she said. "*You* called *me!*"

That got everyone's attention, so of course the room went silent.

"Well, I ... uh, wait a sec, is this Mrs. Belgarden?" Betts's frown switched to a smile at once. "No, this is Betts.... It's my cell phone number.... Oh, I bet you thought maybe the call was from that weirdo who's been stalking Shelby. Am I right?"

Naturally, every eye in the room shifted from Betts to me.

As warmth crept up my neck and into my face I saw Betts's expression change to horror as she realized (too late) what she'd done.

Poor Betts. Even when she tries to, she can't keep a secret!

CHAPTER THIRTEEN

The second Betts hung up the phone everyone started talking to me at once. Even Ms. Lubowski had a question, though I couldn't really hear it in the jumble of voices. I didn't have to, though, because they were all basically the same.

"Someone is *stalking* you?"

I thought frantically, but couldn't come up with a single thing to say that would squash what was almost certainly going to be instant gossip. I could practically hear it racing through Little River phone lines — that ugly word rushing from mouth to mouth: stalker!

Betts decided to help. Unfortunately, I couldn't stop her.

"Well, it's kind of a secret, if you know what I mean," she said. Then she smiled almost flirtatiously. "So maybe you guys shouldn't, like, say anything about it to anyone."

Right.

"And, anyway, we don't even know who it is yet."

Oh, great. Add intrigue to the story. Much better.

"Besides, the police are supposed to have the whole thing solved today, so, in any case, it's probably almost over with now."

I looked at Betts in disbelief. The police are supposed to have the whole thing *solved today*? What did she think the stalker's reaction would be if he heard that? Our biggest hope in catching him was if he slipped up. Word that the police were closing in wasn't likely to make him careless.

I took a couple of steps to where Betts was standing and held out my hand.

"Give me your phone," I said.

She passed it over without hesitation. I got just a smidgen of satisfaction seeing that she looked, well, kind of scared. I flipped the phone open and dialled home.

"Mom, could you pick me up now?" I said as soon as I heard my mother's voice.

"Of course, dear. I'll be right there. Wait for me at the *front entrance*, though."

"Okay," I said. I didn't think much about that, occupied as I was with other thoughts, but I usually got picked up at the side entrance, not the front. That was just habit, since the front is prohibited during times that buses are coming or leaving.

I slung my book bag over my shoulder, told Ms. Lubowski I needed to leave (as if she wasn't already aware of that) and walked from the auditorium. All of my concentration went into keeping my knees from shaking, but I'm not sure I was entirely successful at that.

Mom drove up just as I got to the front door. I slid into the car and she gave me a sympathetic look and asked, "So, was anyone else around when I was talking to Betts?"

"The whole drama club. And yes, they all heard her mention a stalker."

"That's too bad. But you know she didn't mean to let it slip."

"No, I know that." I tried to sound more forgiving than I felt at the moment. I was glad I had a good reason to change the subject. "So, did the police find out where the e-mail was sent from?"

"Yes." Her face was grim and I knew before she went on that it wasn't going to be good news. She took a deep breath and said, "It was sent from the computer lab at the school."

"*My* school? But, how...." I couldn't quite form the questions that were gathering in my head.

"You're wondering how someone got into the school when it would have been locked up by the time that message was sent."

"Yes."

"The side door had been tampered with. Someone

jammed a piece of metal into the catch so that even when the door was fully closed it wasn't latched."

"The side door." I realized with a jolt why she'd wanted to pick me up at the front entrance. Then something else occurred to me. "But Webster went out that door last night. Wouldn't he have noticed something was wrong with it?"

"Who's Webster?"

"The author guy who comes to our book club sometimes." I hesitated, and then told her about his strange behaviour lately.

"Do you think it could be him?" Mom's voice sounded horrified and hopeful all at the same time.

"Webster?" The very idea struck me as ludicrous. "No way." We'd pulled into our driveway by then and I slid from the car still thinking about it. "At least, I don't think so."

"When he left by that exit after your meeting last night, was he on foot?" Mom unlocked the door and pushed it open, then stood back and waited for me to go into the house ahead of her.

"No. He was driving his car." I relocked the door behind me and dropped my book bag onto the floor. "So there's no way it could be him. Whoever heard me talking to Greg couldn't have been in a car. For one thing, we'd have noticed it for sure."

"But he could have parked somewhere and hidden

94

near the house."

"I don't think so. I mean, I know it's possible, but I just can't picture Webster doing that."

Mom touched my arm and then ran her hand along my face in a gentle stroke. She was looking at me like she might cry, which made *me* feel like crying. "I understand that you feel that way, but I think we should mention it to the police anyway."

I wasn't exactly keen on the thought of doing that, especially knowing that Webster was already having problems. And what if he thought I was accusing him of something?

I knew there was no sense in arguing about it, and anyway, what if I was wrong? It could be him. It wasn't impossible. And he *had* been acting strange, and had even given me that odd look last evening.

Mom called the police and told them she had some information and asked if they needed to come by or if she could just give it to them over the phone. When she hung up the phone she told me they were coming right over.

"The officer said this is their highest priority case right now," she said quietly, slipping an arm around my shoulder.

It was Officer Holt who showed up moments later and, oddly enough, I was a bit disappointed it wasn't Mueller. I guess the way he'd handled things after the e-mail gave me confidence in him, even though he'd been sceptical the time before.

Holt and Mom and I sat in the kitchen and he started out by asking me how I was doing. I wasn't sure how to answer that, so I just said I was okay.

"Now, you have some new information?" he asked, flipping his notepad open.

"Mom thinks it might be important," I said. I hoped that conveyed that I didn't, and that I was only telling him this to humour her.

"Mothers are very often right," he said.

"Shelby has good instincts," Mom said, to my surprise. "But this is a bit close to home, if you know what I mean, so she may not be seeing things as clearly as she normally would."

"Sure, sure," he said. He nodded and smiled at me reassuringly. "Thing is, with an investigation like this, the best idea is to give us all the information you can, and let us sort it out from there. Something might not seem important to you, but it could be useful to us."

So I told him about how Webster had been acting a bit unusual at the book club, and that he'd left the school last evening by the side entrance. I felt like a traitor the whole time I was talking, especially after reproaching Jimmy about that very thing that morning.

"You did just right in telling me about this," Officer Holt told me. "Now, don't you worry about a thing. We'll take care of it."

I forced a smile and said thank you.

"There's something else I've been meaning to mention," Mom said. "As I'm sure you know, Shelby has been instrumental in solving a number of crimes here in Little River in the past. Do you think maybe someone is doing this to her as some kind of payback?"

"Doesn't seem like the kind of thing a person would do who was looking for revenge," Officer Holt said. "And the fact that this person has easy access to the school makes it unlikely that it's an outsider, but I'll look into that just the same."

They went over the details of the cases I'd had some luck in solving and Holt jotted down a few things. Then Mom saw him to the door and I went and called Greg and told him the news. It was only after we'd talked that I thought to check the callers list (I'm not yet used to having call display like everyone else in the free world) and when I did, Betts's cell phone number reminded me of what had happened at school.

I glanced at my watch. Drama club should be out by now. Maybe I should call her, I thought. She's probably sick about what she did, and afraid to phone me.

I dialled the number and it rang six times before she answered.

"Hey, Betts."

"Shelby!" She didn't exactly sound penitent. In fact, she sounded excited and happy. "You won't believe what happened!"

"What?"

"Kevin asked me if I wanted to go to a party next weekend!"

Not quite the apology I'd been expecting.

"It's going to be at Tyrone Breau's place, back at Standover Ridge. Hey! Maybe you and Greg can come, too. Oh! That reminds me, you can tell Greg I probably won't need his help after all. So, what do you think? Do you guys want to come?"

"I don't think so. But that's really great news. Good for you."

"Well, it's not an actual date or anything. I mean, he didn't ask me to go with him. It was more like a, 'Hey, if you're not doing anything you should come' kind of thing. But it's still a good sign, don't you think?"

"Yeah, sure. It's definitely a good sign."

"Oh!" Her voice changed, dropping from excited to serious. "I'm so sorry. I forgot to ask you what the police found out. I was just so …"

"I know. Don't worry about it. Anyway, all they found out is that the e-mail came from … uh … a public place. So, no help there." I said a few more vague things and told her I was real happy for her about Kevin. Then, pleading a ton of homework, I told her I'd see her the next day.

I think you can probably understand why I didn't give her specific details!

CHAPTER FOURTEEN

We'd just finished eating dinner that evening when the phone rang. Normally, I'd be the one to jump up and go answer it, but lately I was finding myself tensing up inside when it rang. When Dad hurried toward the kitchen, it was just one more reminder that my life wasn't exactly normal at the moment.

He came back after a few minutes, his face serious.

"That was Alyson Stark," he said.

"Looking for a story?" Mom asked.

"What else?"

Alyson Stark is a reporter for the local paper. She's also Nora Stark's mother, and Nora is in the drama club. I couldn't specifically remember seeing her at today's meeting, but she must have been there.

"What did you tell her?"

"I told her we'd think about it and let her know."

I was surprised that Dad had told her we'd even consider giving her a story, and my surprise must have shown on my face, since he immediately began to explain.

"Alyson pointed out that the story is going to get around anyway, and she said there are a few things we should think about before we decide if we want it in the paper.

"For one thing, it might help keep rumours from getting out of hand. You know how things grow and get exaggerated around here."

I nodded at that. I'd seen it a lot in the last year or so, but it wasn't usually focused directly on me. I have to say it was a whole lot worse knowing that people would be talking about me, spreading stories that were bound to get wilder and wilder as they were twisted and embellished.

"And it could help catch this idiot."

"How?"

"By having the whole town — and especially this neighbourhood — on the alert. If everyone around is watching for anyone or anything suspicious, someone is bound to see something."

"That isn't *always* a good thing," Mom said. When Dad and I both looked at her questioningly, she explained. "Well, the police could be swamped with calls. If their time is wasted looking into every person who happens to walk along a sidewalk in our neighbourhood, they'll be so busy they might not have time to check legitimate leads."

"That might happen anyway, once the rumours get around," I said.

We went over the pros and cons for a while, and then they asked me what I thought.

"You're letting me decide?" I said in surprise.

"Not exactly," Dad admitted. "We have to make whatever decision we believe is best, but we'd like to know how you feel so we can consider it along with everything else."

"I think we should go ahead," I said, relieved I wasn't actually calling the shot.

"So do I," Mom said. I knew she was reluctant about it, considering the possible drawbacks, but, like me, she saw more good than bad in the idea.

"It's unanimous, then." Dad got up and headed back to the kitchen. "I'll give Alyson a call and tell her she can come over."

Mrs. Stark must have had her keys in her hands, waiting for Dad's call, because she drove into our driveway less than ten minutes after he let her know we'd decided to give her the details. She burst into the kitchen trying to keep her face solemn, though there was a spark of excitement in her eyes. I suppose that's what makes for a good reporter: feeling the thrill of a story even if it's about something bad.

"Shelby, *honey,*" she said to me, though I don't think we'd ever actually met before, "I was just *horrified* when Nora told me about this. I mean, this is Little River, right? Things like this just don't *happen* here."

"Would you prefer to sit in the living room or here in the kitchen?" Mom asked, keeping her voice neutral. Even so, I could tell immediately that she didn't like the breezy way Mrs. Stark was acting.

"Wherever Shelby is more comfortable," she said.

"I'm afraid we're not quite on the same page here, Alyson," Dad interrupted. "You won't be interviewing Shelby."

"Oh?" Her eyebrows shot up like he'd just said the most surprising thing ever.

"No. You'll be talking to me and my wife, and no one else." Dad's voice and expression were both mild, and I wondered if Mrs. Stark would try to persuade him to let her talk to me. If she did, she'd see that his tone and appearance were both deceptive.

She went for a different tactic. "Well, *of course*, whatever you think is best. We'll just get a couple of quick shots of Shelby and then she can run off and do whatever she likes." A camera materialized in her hand as if by magic. "If she's anything like Nora, she probably has a *truckload* of homework to get done anyway."

"There won't be any pictures," Dad said. Same voice, same look. "Darlene and I will give you the details of what's happened and that will be it."

"Are you sure about this? I mean, not everyone knows what Shelby looks like. It would be helpful for them to see her. Otherwise there could be calls left, right, and centre about every teenaged girl who happens to be walking down the street with a boy anywhere near her."

"No pictures," Dad answered evenly. "The neighbours all know Shelby, and they're the ones who are most likely to see and report anything suspicious."

I saw her weigh whether or not to push any harder for the picture. Maybe she sensed that, if she argued about it any more, she'd blow the whole thing. In any case, she put her bright smile back on and said of course she understood and whatever they thought was best would be just fine.

"So, there definitely *won't* be a picture of Shelby in the paper," Mom said. "I have no doubt you could dig one up somewhere, so I just want it really clear what we've agreed to. I want your word on this."

The smile never left Mrs. Stark's face, but it wavered, ever so slightly, for a fraction of a second. "You have my word," she said. "No picture."

That satisfied my parents and the three of them sat down at the kitchen table. A tablet and tape recorder appeared, but Mrs. Stark hesitated before she started to ask questions.

It hit me that she'd expected my parents to send me

103

out of the room or something, and that her hesitation was to give them a chance to do that. As if! My folks wouldn't dream of treating me that way. I knew it was up to me if I wanted to stick around or not. I actually had no interest in hearing the whole thing rehashed, but I stayed for a few minutes anyway before heading to my room to get at my homework.

When I turned on the light, the first thing I noticed was that the curtain was open. Without thinking, I switched the light back off, crossed the room, and yanked the curtains closed. Even so, I decided to use my desk lamp because the brighter overhead light was more likely to show a silhouette of me when I passed the window.

I wondered if he was out there, watching. I wondered if he'd seen what I'd just done, and if he had, how it made him feel. Powerful? Amused? Angry? It was impossible to guess what this guy's reaction might be, although it would be a safe bet that it wasn't normal.

Did he know I was afraid? Would he like that, or would he be angry that he hadn't somehow won me over?

It was horrible to have every move I made governed by fear. Unless you've experienced something like this, you really can't imagine what it's like.

As I booted my computer, I wondered what I'd done that had first gotten this person's attention. Nothing was different about me. If anything, I could be considered a bit on the boring side. I go to school every week, to church every Sunday. I spend time with my boyfriend and my friends doing very ordinary things. And that pretty much describes my life. Ordinary.

A thought struck me then. The only thing I'd done that was at all different from other years was join the drama and book clubs at school.

I picked up the notepad I'd been using to write down everything that this guy had done, and drew a line down the centre of one page. It might be a good idea to make a list of the guys in the two clubs. Just in case.

Drama Club	**Book Club**
Kevin Montoya	Bruce Kerr
Edison Hale	Jason Puckett
Tyrone Breau	Jimmy Roth
Jimmy Farrell	Ben Hebert
Jimmy Roth	Greg Taylor
Ben Hebert	Webster (not a student)
Eric Green	
Darren Fischer	

I felt a bit silly once I'd written down the names. I mean, what was a list of names going to tell me? I already knew who was in each group, and that a couple of the guys were in both groups.

Actually, picturing each guy in my head, it seemed less likely that the stalker was one of them. These were all just regular guys. Nothing strange about any of them.

Well, Betts had mentioned that Eric had asked if I was still going out with Greg, but that was nothing. Even so, I made a note about it on a separate page.

I glanced over the list again, shoved it into my desk drawer, and turned to my computer. I almost opted against going online and checking my e-mails, but the thought that this guy was starting to control an awful lot of things I did really made me angry.

I logged onto my account and only flinched a little when there was a message from an unknown sender. Luckily, it was just junk mail. I relaxed, glad I'd gone ahead.

The less power I give him, the better, I thought. He won't know it, but *I* will.

CHAPTER FIFTEEN

As you can imagine, when the paper came out with the story about the stalker, it was pretty big news. Little River, like most small towns, is generally peaceful, quiet, and law-abiding. The idea that there was a crime of this sort going on right in their own town was more excitement than most Little River residents have had in a long while.

I, however, was anything but overjoyed to be the focal point of the story. All I could hope was that they'd catch the guy soon, at which time the attention would almost certainly shift over to him.

I'd have preferred to stay home as much as possible, but with Christmas just around the corner I had no choice but to go out quite often. And everywhere I went there were whispers behind my back. Hushed conversations that might have fooled me if it wasn't for the corresponding fingers that were inevitably pointing in my direction.

"That's her," I'd hear. Or, "There she is!" as if they'd been out looking for me all day or something.

Then they'd try to pretend they weren't talking about me. Their heads would stop swivelling with every step I took, but I could still feel the eyes following me. And the second I left a store or whatever, I could hear voices rising in excited chatter.

I hated it. And there wasn't a thing I could do about it. But, I have to admit, it got me feeling just a little safer, too. After all, it would be pretty hard for anyone to make a move on me with the whole town's eyes looking on.

In spite of the newspaper's factual reporting (and, as promised, no picture) there were still some wild stories flying around. I even overheard one of them when I was at the library looking for a book on Sir Frederick Banting. The conversation was taking place in the book aisle behind where I was standing, and the elderly ladies who were talking clearly had no idea that I was right there within earshot of their gossip.

"It's hard to believe we have a stalker right here in Little River," one woman said in a loud whisper. "I've barely been able to sleep at night since I heard about it."

"I know, I know. A person hardly feels safe in their own home anymore," the second agreed.

While I wondered what they thought *they* had to be nervous about, I heard the sounds of a book dropping and being retrieved.

"I heard that this fellow's been sending the little Belgarden girl flowers and candy every day, but the police won't say whether or not any of the candy was poisoned."

"*I* heard the candy was sent to her boyfriend. Supposedly from *her*. And he was just about to eat a piece when his dog bumped him and it dropped. And what do you think but the dog gobbled it down and fell over dead. Saved the boy's life!"

"You don't say!"

"I *do* say! Now, you can't tell me that dog didn't know what it was doing."

"I like cats myself, though I don't suppose my Whimsy would sacrifice herself for me that way."

The embarrassment I'd felt when the women began talking had changed to disbelief and then to anger. I took a few quick steps out, around, and into the aisle they occupied. Neither woman was familiar to me.

"Good afternoon, ladies," I said. I tried to sound pleasant and unperturbed, the way Mom does when she's upset and hiding it.

"Oh, hello," one answered. Both smiled at me quizzically.

"My name," I said, smiling back, "is Shelby Belgarden, and I just happened to hear your conversation

... about me. I thought maybe you should know that I've never *received* candy from the person who's been bothering me. Neither has my boyfriend Greg, who, incidentally, does not even *have* a dog."

Their mouths fell open but neither spoke.

"I don't mean to be rude, but this whole thing is difficult enough for me without people spreading this kind of ridiculous gossip."

I turned and walked away, and then headed for the section Mom was browsing while she waited for me. You'd think I'd have felt a whole lot better after getting that out, but I didn't. I felt mean and horrid, like I'd just picked on a couple of harmless old ladies for no good reason.

I worried about Webster too, and hoped that no one would connect the visit he'd received from the police to the stalking story. I hadn't heard anything along those lines, at least, and I was thankful for that, because it seemed the poor man already had enough problems without people thinking that of him.

In a lot of ways, school was worse than anything. A lot of kids were sympathetic and supportive, but others seemed to think it was something to joke about. They'd call out to any guy who happened to be walking behind me and ask him moronic things, such as was he stalking me.

But even harder to take were the snide remarks I'd hear — mostly from girls. It wasn't so much *what* they'd say as the *way* they'd say it. Their comments made it sound as though I'd manufactured the entire story for attention — the last thing I'd actually want!

I couldn't do anything but swallow my anger and humiliation and hope they felt like dirt when they found out how wrong they'd been.

And then there was the worst thing of all: whoever the stalker was, he was almost certainly a student at Little River High. The fact that the e-mail had been sent from the school meant he had to have been inside in the daytime and had an opportunity to jimmy the lock on the side door. Any outsider would have been noticed.

He also had to know where the computer lab was and what time the building was deserted in the evenings. And, of course, he had to have been around me in order to have developed this bizarre obsession.

Then something else happened — something horrible — and it removed any hint of doubt I might have had that the stalker was a fellow student.

I'd been so wrapped up in how awful it was for *me* that I'd forgotten something. This jerk had threatened to do something to Greg. I guess none of us had taken that very seriously, which strikes me as odd, looking back on it. But it just seemed, at the time, to be nonsense. And then there was the fact that we didn't know just how sick and dangerous he really was.

My fears centred on being followed, watched, possibly approached by this guy. I never thought of him doing anything really hurtful. The idea that he could be seriously violent seemed melodramatic and totally over-the-top.

It happened on a Tuesday, right after school, when the hallways and locker areas were crowded with kids who were anxious to head out, to breathe outside air after being stuck inside all day.

Like so many other students, I was fishing through my locker, making sure I had the books I needed for my homework, getting my jacket on — just doing what we do every school day.

I wasn't even alarmed when I first heard the screams. It's not that unusual, especially after school when everyone's energy has been pent up all day. It sounded like the shrieks you might hear in reaction to a silly, scary trick.

But the sound changed fast. It swelled with real alarm and panic. I stood frozen with the sudden certainty that, somehow, this had something to do with the stalker.

Everything slowed down, as though sounds and movements had been stretched. I became aware of a heavy thudding in my chest. My brain was struggling to put the surge of thoughts together, and when it did I heard a low, frightened moan, and knew it had come from me.

No one had to tell me — somehow I just knew! Something had happened to Greg!

CHAPTER SIXTEEN

Getting to Greg's locker felt like one of those slow-motion dreams you have where you're trying to hurry but your whole body feels as though it's weighed down with lead. As I manoeuvred my way down the hallway I felt a wave of nausea, and small dark clouds began to form in my field of vision.

Don't faint! I told myself sternly, but I knew I was going to if I didn't do something to stop it that very second. Those warning signs couldn't be ignored. I paused and squatted, putting my head down and breathing deeply. It was the hardest thing: to stop and do that when everything in me was screaming to hurry up and get to Greg.

I forced myself to stay that way for a good two or three minutes, though every second that ticked past was an agony of waiting. When I stood again I came face-to-face with Ben Hebert.

"You okay?" he asked. "You look kinda pale."

"I felt faint, but I think I'm okay now. Thanks," I said. I nodded toward the sounds of the commotion and began walking that way. "I have to see what's going on."

"Yeah, I was on my way there when I saw you bent over," he said, falling in beside me. After a moment or two he said, "You can take my arm if you need to."

"I'm all right," I said impatiently. We were almost there by then. Just a few more steps to the next hall where the grade twelve students had their lockers.

The sight that met my eyes when I turned that corner is one I will never be able to forget. Greg stood surrounded by other students, some of who seemed to be holding him up. Blood almost covered his face and I might not even have known for sure that it was him except for the fact that I recognized the shirt he was wearing.

"Greg!" I tried to push my way forward through the growing crowd, but no one was budging.

"Please, keep back! An ambulance is on the way."

I recognized that voice as Mr. Grimes's and saw that there were several other teachers there as well. Their efforts to keep order weren't meeting with much success.

"Greg!" I called out again, and saw his head turn toward me slightly.

"Shelby?" His right hand lifted in a little wave, which brought tears to my eyes. "Hey, can you let her through, please?"

At least the kids listened to *him*, and I was ushered through the crowd.

"It's nothing, *really*," he said when I got close enough to touch his arm. "It probably looks bad, but I'm okay."

My throat was tight and aching so fiercely that I couldn't speak. I stood silently, squeezing his arm and trying not to break down sobbing in front of everyone. Other things began to register, like that a couple of other kids were also bleeding, though not nearly as much as Greg. And there were shards of glass all over the floor.

I tried to ask what had happened but the pandemonium was growing and more and more people were arriving on the scene, creating so much noise that my voice was lost in it all. It seemed that half the people there were talking to Greg — asking him questions, telling him things like "keep pressure on the cuts" and so on.

The ambulance arrived just a moment later and, in spite of his protests that it wasn't necessary, Greg was taken to the hospital. As the ambulance workers strapped him to the stretcher he told me that he'd call me later.

"Don't waste your time coming to the hospital," he said. "I'll be out before you know it."

As if! I phoned home and Mom came at once and drove me straight to the emergency department. I hurried in while she parked the car.

A nurse directed me to the examining room he was in and, finding the door open, I stepped inside. Another nurse was there, cleaning the blood away from his face.

"Yes?" she asked, turning to me.

"What did I tell you?" Greg said before I could answer. "That's my girlfriend, Shelby."

"Oh, yes." The nurse smiled. "Greg was just saying that you never listen to him, so you should be arriving any minute."

"She's a walking advertisement for the modern, liberated woman, that Shelby," he commented.

"How bad is it?" I asked, ignoring his teasing.

"I'd say he was pretty lucky, considering," the nurse said. "There are a couple of cuts that will need stitches, but mostly they're superficial wounds."

"But there was *so* much blood," I said. "His whole face was covered."

"Mmm. Scalp wounds are like that. They bleed like crazy. He actually doesn't have any cuts on his face. A few small ones high on the forehead and the deeper ones on the scalp. Could have been worse."

"What happened?" I asked Greg.

"I don't really know. I opened my locker and the next thing I knew I was bleeding. I felt something

116

smash into my head but I was looking down at the books I was holding, so I didn't really see anything." He shrugged, like it was no big deal.

"You have no idea who did this? You didn't see anyone coming at you?"

"No one came at me," he said. "It came from inside my locker."

"From inside your locker? But how…?"

"Someone booby-trapped it, I guess. And it had to be spring-loaded because it came out with quite a bit of force. You probably noticed that I wasn't the only one who got cut. My guess is that someone rigged a bunch of broken glass on the shelf so that it would fly out when the door was opened."

"It's just fortunate he had his head down," the nurse commented. "If he'd been hit in the face he could have ended up all scarred. And you don't even want to *think* about what it could have done to his eyes."

I shuddered at that, and I saw that Greg looked pretty solemn too.

"I'd like to know what kind of monster would *do* something like this," the nurse added. "I suppose it's the one they wrote about in the paper. Well, I hope they catch the guy soon. Bad enough he's making *your* life miserable," she said with a glance at me, "but this! This is no joke."

I hadn't thought what the stalker was doing to me was exactly a joke either, but I knew what she meant. Getting phone calls or e-mails or being watched is one thing; actually being injured is something else again.

The doctor came along and sent me out while he stitched up the deep cuts. I found Mom in the waiting area and sat down next to her. While we waited, I told her about how Greg's locker had been booby-trapped. Just as I finished going over the whole thing, Greg came along, smiling and saying he was good to go.

"Oh! Oh my goodness!" Mom said, looking at him in horror. I guess hearing about what had happened hadn't really prepared her for the stitched gashes on his head (clearly visible since they'd shaved those spots) or the sight of the drying blood all over his shirt. I hadn't even realized myself how much blood had run down. It looked pretty bad.

"I'm fine," Greg told Mom. "Just a few nicks, really."

"Has anyone called your father?"

"Nah. He's in Viander today and anyway, there's no reason for him to come rushing home or anything."

"Well, I think he'd want to be told," Mom said. She looked worried. "I know *I'd* want to be contacted if it was Shelby."

"I'll call him if you really think I should," Greg said slowly, "but then he's just going to be worrying driving home."

"You're right. I don't know what's best now!"

In the end it was decided that Greg would call his dad and tell him he'd gotten cut a bit and had to have stitches, and that we thought he should come over to our place until his dad got him, just to be on the safe side. It went fine until Dr. Taylor asked to speak to Mom.

"Yes, Malcolm, how are you?" she said. "Yes, Greg is fine. I just thought he could stay with us until you get home. Okay then, we'll see you later on."

"You might as well expect to see my dad in about forty minutes," Greg said as we piled into the car. "He'll be leaving Viander right about now."

"But I didn't give anything away," Mom protested.

"Not in what you said," Greg smiled, "but your voice wasn't exactly steady. No way Dad missed that. He knows there's more to it than what we told him."

"In that case," Mom said, "I'll just make enough dinner to include Malcolm, too."

Sure enough, Greg's dad pulled into our driveway a little over half an hour after we got home. If the thought that he might be overreacting had ever entered his head, it probably vanished once he saw the police cruiser in the driveway.

CHAPTER SEVENTEEN

It was Dr. Taylor who suggested that I look to see if the stalker had sent any more messages.

"From a professional view of this person," he said, "I'd say it would be almost impossible for him not to make *sure* you know he's responsible for what happened to Greg."

"Hey, that's right, you're a shri...er, a psychiatrist, aren't you?" Officer Holt said. He, along with Officer Stanton, had responded to this particular call.

"A psychologist, actually," Dr. Taylor said. He turned back to me. "Would you like someone to come with you while you check your e-mail?"

"Could Officer Stanton come?" I said quickly, before either of my parents could say anything. I didn't want them, or Greg, to be with me when I opened my e-mail account. It just seemed as if it would be easier with a stranger there.

Officer Stanton stood behind me while my computer whirred to life, waiting silently as I went online and into my e-mail account. I scanned the new e-mails, most of them stuff friends had forwarded. His was third from the last, sent at 3:24 that afternoon. The entire message was one line long.

Now you see what happens when you trifle with me.

"Print it," Stanton said.

I did as she'd asked and watched the sheet feed out into the printer tray. Officer Stanton picked it up and then rested a hand on my shoulder.

"I know this must be rough on you," she said quietly. "But we *will* catch this guy."

"Yeah, thanks." I knew as well as she did that this creep was going to have to make a mistake before they'd ever figure out his identity, and so far he'd been careful. It didn't take much brainpower to guess that today's e-mail would have been sent from the school, just like the last one.

We went back to the other room, where our entrance was met with instant silence. Everyone was looking at me; everyone's face had the same question on it.

"You were right," I told Dr. Taylor. "He sent a message."

"It was short," Officer Stanton said. She lifted the printout and read it. "'Now you see what happens when you trifle with me.'"

Dr. Taylor nodded. "This person is taking increased risks," he said. "He went from carefully covering his tracks with the plant delivery to taking a huge chance in setting up a booby trap in Greg's locker. This means he's either becoming more desperate, or he's developing a sense of invincibility."

"Which do you think it is?" Dad asked.

"I couldn't venture a guess. Either scenario, this is a dangerous person. I don't think either Shelby or Greg should be left alone at any time until this person is in custody."

He looked at the page again and added, "Something else that suggests this person feels powerful is the name he's chosen for himself."

"You mean 'soreros' is a real name?" Stanton asked.

"Not as it appears," Dr. Taylor said, "but it looks as though he's barely hidden the name of Eros, the Greek God of love and desire, in there. If you start at the centre of the word it reads Eros backward to the start and forward to the end."

He was about to say something else when the phone rang. Officer Holt went with Mom into the kitchen to answer it. A few seconds later Mom came to the doorway and beckoned for me.

"*It's him,*" she whispered, "but the officer thinks you should talk to him. See if he says anything that might give away his identity."

I followed her, my stomach clenching as I approached the phone.

"Hello."

"Shelby." It was the same whisper as before.

"Who is this?" I demanded, knowing I was letting my anger take over, knowing that was a mistake, and powerless to stop myself.

There was a soft chuckle, like I'd just said something amusing. I guess I had, by asking him who he was as if he might actually tell me. Then I realized it wasn't the question, but the anger behind it, that was giving him such a kick. He'd heard the emotion in my voice and was enjoying it.

"Not so pleasant to look at now, is he?" he said after a second of silence.

"Who? Greg?"

"Yes, Greg. Or," another horrible chuckle, "maybe we should call him Scarface."

"Listen. Whoever you are and whatever you want, please leave him alone. He hasn't done anything to you."

"Ah, Shelby. You still don't understand. *You're* the one who caused this. I told you to break up with him, but you didn't listen. You still haven't seen the truth."

"And what is the truth?"

"I won't repeat myself."

A click sounded, startling me. I turned to Officer Holt. "He hung up," I said. "Sorry."

"You did fine," he assured me. "Now, before anything else, write down everything he said the best you can remember it."

I did that, scribbling quickly before his words faded, though at that moment I suspected I wouldn't be able to get them out of my head if I tried.

"Oh!" I said, pausing for a second. "I forgot to check the phone to see if it said where he was calling from. Or to press star fifty-seven to trace it, if it doesn't show."

Mom glanced away from me.

"What? What is it?" I knew immediately that there was something she didn't want to tell me.

"The call," she said heavily, "came from the Taylor house."

"*What*? From *Greg's* place?"

"Yes. The police radioed for a car to swing by their house, but I imagine he'll be long gone by the time they get there."

I went into the other room, where Officer Holt was telling Dr. Taylor and Greg that the call had been from the perpetrator and that it had come from inside their house.

"Well," Dr. Taylor said with a rueful smile, "that answers the question of what's motivating him."

"How?" Officer Holt asked.

"He has no reason to break into our house to make the call when he could have done it from a public phone with very little risk to himself. Instead, he's chanced being seen by a neighbour entering or leaving our home. Or, we could have walked in at any time and caught him. He's also taken a chance on leaving forensic evidence behind with no way to explain how it got there. Those aren't acts of desperation. They're acts of bravado. He feels invincible, like no one can catch him. Fortunately, it's that very sense of omnipotence that will probably be his downfall."

I was only half listening to what Dr. Taylor was saying, even though it was about the stalker. Knowing that this guy had been inside their house when he'd called really scared me. I couldn't understand why everyone else wasn't thinking of all the possibilities that went along with that.

For instance, what if he'd done something there, too: set another booby-trap, destroyed things ... or even worse?

"How can we be sure that the house is safe for Greg and Dr. Taylor to go back to?" I worried aloud.

"We'll check that out *very* carefully," Officer Stanton said.

"Can we be in the house while you're looking around?" Dr. Taylor wanted to know.

"It might be best if you aren't, just in case," Officer Holt said.

"You and Greg will have dinner here, of course," Mom said to Dr. Taylor. "And the police can let you know when they're through."

So, the Taylors stayed for dinner, but it wasn't a happy meal. Everyone was trying to act normal, and to pretend that Greg didn't look like Frankenstein with his head shaved and stitched in three places.

I kept thinking that his injuries could have been so much worse if he hadn't happened to have his head down when he opened his locker door. And I wondered what the police would find when they went into the Taylor house, and what this guy had in store next. Would he target Greg again, or me, or maybe my parents?

It all felt like my fault, somehow, though I knew that wasn't true. Then something occurred to me. At first it seemed unthinkable, but after only a few moments I knew it was the best thing to do.

"Greg, I need to speak to you," I said after we'd all eaten and the table had been cleared.

He followed me to the TV room and waited, sensing the gravity of my mood.

"This has all gotten too heavy for me," I said, forcing my voice to stay even. "With everything that's going on, I just don't have the energy for a relationship anymore. I'm sorry."

"You're breaking up with me?" His voice was disbelieving. "Are you serious?"

"Yes."

"You're giving in to this jerk?" he said.

"No, it's not that." But it *was* that. It was the only thing I knew to do that would protect Greg.

"You think he'll back off if you aren't going out with me," he stated. His voice was flat, and I realized he'd been carrying a pretty heavy load himself.

"That's part of it," I admitted. It would be impossible to persuade him otherwise. "But it's not the *only* reason. Everything that's happened has gotten me thinking about a lot of stuff, and this is one of them."

"Meaning *us*?"

"Yeah. Us. I'm sorry, but I can see now that this was coming anyway."

"And by 'this' you mean us breaking up?" All the time we were talking he kept looking right at me. I wished he'd stop.

"Yes." The truth was that all I wanted was to throw my arms around him and tell him I *never* wanted to break up. But if I did that, he'd still be in danger. I knew I couldn't live with myself if something happened to Greg because I wasn't strong enough to do what I knew had to be done.

"To be perfectly honest," I said, "I've been wanting to break up for a while. This just gave me the excuse I needed."

He said nothing for a moment. He just kept staring at me with a look on his face like he was trying to figure out if he'd imagined the whole conversation. When he did speak again, all he said was, "You mean that?"

"Yeah," I said. "I do."

He shrugged, as if to say, "what can you do?" and then he walked out of the room.

And that was it. We were through.

CHAPTER EIGHTEEN

I slept very little that night. Once, around three in the morning, with Ernie snuggled in and purring beside me, it struck me that at least fear wasn't the main thing I was feeling anymore.

On the other hand, I can't say that I recommend heartbreak as a terrific substitute. I told myself over and over that I had no choice, but it didn't help.

It's Greg's fault, I told myself once, as the tears swelled and spilled over. If I'd thought I could have persuaded him to *pretend* we'd broken up, I would have, but I knew there was no way he would go along with that. Greg isn't the type to back down from anything — least of all some kind of threat.

The only way I could hope to convince the stalker that I'd broken up with Greg was if I'd actually done it.

The worst thing about it was knowing I'd hurt Greg. It had actually stunned me to see how quickly he'd believed that I'd been wanting to end things anyway. Nothing in the world could be further from the truth and it was a shock that he hadn't known that.

I told myself over and over that when the stalker had been caught and everything was back to normal, I could go to Greg and tell him the truth. Surely there'd be a good chance that we'd get back together. But part of me knew it wouldn't be that easy. Greg can be stubborn sometimes, and finding out that I'd felt I had to protect him was going to hurt his pride. Besides, whatever he was feeling right now was real, and I wasn't sure he'd be that eager to forgive me for putting him through it.

I'd gone around everything a hundred times by morning but I can't say I felt any better. I was exhausted and my head ached as I crawled out of bed and headed for the shower. The temptation to stay home was strong, but I couldn't. I needed to get to school and get the word out. Until the stalker heard — and *believed* — that I'd broken up with him, Greg wasn't safe.

I'm sure my folks noticed that something was wrong, but they didn't ask me anything. No doubt they just thought I was worried and worn down from the whole business. They had no reason to think there was a problem with Greg.

Dad drove me to school and waited until I joined Betts before driving away. She was exactly the person I needed just then!

"Hey, Shelby." Her usual morning greeting.

"Hey," I made sure my voice dragged despondently. That got her attention, just as I'd known it would.

"Is something wrong?"

"Uh, yeah, you could say that." Don't be too anxious, I told myself. Make her drag it out of you or she'll be suspicious. Betts is pretty sharp when it comes to stuff like this.

"Is it the stalker thing?" Her voice was full of sympathy.

"Well, that's part of it, yeah."

"What else?"

"I don't really feel much like talking about it," I said. The idea that I was holding out on her would only make Betts determined to dig it out of me.

I let her cajole and prod for a few more minutes while we made our way to our lockers. Then, with my voice trembling, I told her that Greg and I had broken up.

"I don't believe it!" she said. I thought I'd blown it, but then I realized she hadn't meant what she'd said literally. "I thought you guys were solid, like you were *never* going to break up," she said, shaking her head. "What happened?"

I told her I wasn't up to talking about it. She asked who'd done the breaking up — the question girls *always* ask when a couple splits — and I said I had.

"To be, like, brutally honest with you, Shelby, you don't look all that happy about it," she said.

"Well, I'm not, but I know it was the right decision." At least that was one hundred percent true.

"Is this about what happened to Greg yesterday?"

"No."

She looked sceptical. I knew I had to convince her so I basically repeated what I'd told Greg. Only, it was probably easier for Betts to believe all of that, because she could relate it to the way her own relationships often end.

"You think you guys will get back together?" she asked when I was finished.

"I doubt it."

"But you've been together for such a long time!" she protested.

"All the more reason," I said, hardly believing I could make myself say these things. "I'd like to see what it's like to go out with other guys."

Betts nodded, although kind of sadly, still letting it all sink in. Then she asked the magic question.

"Is this, like, a secret or anything?"

"A secret?" I tried to look puzzled. "No. Why would it be?"

"I dunno," she said, "I just thought you might want to keep it quiet or something."

"Nope." I shrugged indifferently to prove it. "I don't care who you tell."

As we each headed off in different directions toward our first classes, I had a pang of anger toward Betts. I knew it was totally unjustified, but it was there anyway. I'd *wanted* her to spread the story about the break-up, and yet there I was, resenting her for it. Maybe if she didn't get so excited about gossip I'd have felt differently.

I told myself that it didn't matter whether she enjoyed it or not, the main thing was that I could count on her to get the word out.

News like that travels quickly, and when the first class ended and we all headed off to our second classes I was already being asked about it.

"Shelby! It's not true about you and Greg splitting up, is it?"

"Yes, it's true." Keep walking, I told myself. Don't start bawling. Act like this is what you want! Somewhere in these halls the stalker is watching.

By noon I could hardly eat my lunch in peace — not that I had much of an appetite anyway. Mostly it was girls, but a couple of guys even asked me if it was true I'd dumped Greg.

Dumped? I thought. What a horrible way to put it. But I told them, yeah, I'd dumped him. I even tried to smile.

133

A few people had unbelievably stupid questions and I amazed myself by not losing it when I answered them. For example, Rhonda O'Neill wanted to know if I'd "caught Greg kissing another girl or anything."

"No, nothing like that," I managed. The idea that she'd even *ask* such a trashy question about someone like Greg infuriated me. Just as insulting, except this time toward me, was Deanna Cline's question.

"Hey, I bet you broke up with Greg because of his hair, right?"

It took me a couple of seconds to realize that she was talking about the shaved places on his head. But even after I understood what she meant, it was still hard to believe anyone would even *think* that.

"Of course not," I snapped, unable to help myself. "What kind of low-life would break up with someone because of something like that?"

"You don't have to call me names," she answered. The unintended admission might have made me laugh if it wasn't so pathetic.

Jimmy Roth wandered by and said, "Like the old saying goes, one man's gain is another man's loss."

"Don't you have that backward?" Betts asked.

"Nope," he said. But he laughed and winked to show he was only teasing. I managed a feeble smile back just in case the stalker was watching.

And Eric Green came over. He didn't say anything

about the break-up, but he looked around and said, "It sure is crowded in here today. I guess I'll just sit with you guys."

Betts took a big bite of her sandwich and chewed vigorously. I could see she was thinking the same thing I was. It was no more crowded than any other day and Eric had never parked himself at our table before.

Thinking about Betts's theory that he liked me, I spent the next twenty minutes in agony. I was scared he was going to ask me out, but he never said another word. He just ate his lunch, staring straight ahead with his face kind of embarrassed looking.

One thing was clear: word was getting around just as fast as I'd hoped. With any luck, the stalker would have heard about the break-up before the end of the day. And even if he had doubts about it, surely he'd wait to see if it was true before he tried to do anything else to hurt Greg.

I thought I could stand anything but that.

CHAPTER NINETEEN

The next few days were pure misery, and the worst part was how I had to put on a happy front — not just at school, but at home, too. I hadn't told my parents about breaking up with Greg because I really didn't know what they'd think about it.

I'd been expecting one of them to ask me about whether the stalker had done anything at the Taylor house the night he'd called from there — the same night I told Greg we were through. I didn't know what I was going to say, but luckily, it was Mom who mentioned it, and it turned out she'd called Dr. Taylor.

"I was speaking with Malcolm earlier," she said casually as we set the table. "Wasn't it fortunate that nothing was damaged or stolen — that they know of, anyway."

Relief flooded over me. "Yeah, that was great," I said. I wondered why she didn't realize how "off" I sounded.

"Well, I'm sure we'll all feel safer with new security systems installed in both homes," she added. Of course, she assumed Greg would have told me that the Taylors were getting that done themselves.

I spent as much time as possible doing homework, and for once I was actually ahead in getting assignments done. No one questioned it, or seemed to notice that anything was wrong.

Even so, it was only a few days until Mom commented that it was odd Greg hadn't called lately.

I was drying the dishes at the time and she really caught me off guard bringing it up out of the blue. I couldn't think of anything to say so I just concentrated on the bunch of silverware I was holding with the tea towel.

"Shelby?" Mom's tone told me she'd finally noticed.

"Huh?"

"Is there anything wrong between you and Greg?"

"We broke up," I said. "But I don't want to talk about it."

That was Mom's cue to ask me a couple of dozen questions, starting with "who" and "why," and ending with "haven't I raised you to be able to talk to me about anything."

I dug in and just kept saying I really didn't feel like discussing it. In the end, all the misery and anger and helplessness built up and burst.

"Why can't you just stop?" I yelled. "I said I don't want to talk about it and I meant *I don't want to talk about it*. I want to be left alone!"

I threw down the cloth and ran from the kitchen to my room, where I slammed the door and flung myself across the bed, sobbing. I was sure Mom would follow me, knock on the door, and ask if she could come in, and I knew that if she did I was going to lose it completely. But she didn't.

I cried until I was so exhausted I could barely move. I wished I could just crawl into bed and sleep for days — weeks, if necessary — and wake up to find this whole mess over with and the stalker caught.

What if it takes them months to find him? I thought. What if they don't find him at all? The last day had been the longest of my life and I didn't know how I was going to get through the rest of the week.

Eventually I forced myself to get up and pull out my homework. It seemed to take forever to do it, even though it was really only a couple of hours. Then I went looking for Mom. I found her in the TV room with Dad, but the set wasn't on. It looked as though they'd been talking, but had stopped when they'd heard me coming.

"I'm sorry," I said. "For yelling at you."

"Oh, no, honey. *I'm* the one who should apologize," Mom said. "It was disrespectful of me to keep pushing when you said you didn't want to talk."

"Yeah, but you can't help yourself," I said. I even managed a little smile.

"It's hard for your mother and me to see you going through all this business," Dad said. "It's hard not to be able to do anything about it. And now, to find out you and Greg are broken up and you're carrying that around, too." He shook his head.

"I didn't want to break up with Greg," I said. "I *had* to do it." Then the whole thing just burst out of me.

"But you can't tell his dad or *anyone*," I said.

They said they wouldn't unless there was some compelling reason that they had to.

After that I hunted around until I found Ernie. He'd come scratching at my door earlier, but I'd been too upset to go and let him in. I felt guilty about it because I knew he'd heard or sensed that I was upset and had wanted to comfort me, the way he always does if something is bothering me.

I found him curled up behind a big planter in the dining room, but he must have been insulted by the earlier rejection because he yawned and acted disinterested in coming to me when I coaxed him.

"Fine," I said, and I walked away. Still, when I went back to my room to get ready for bed, I left the door open just the tiniest amount. I was climbing into bed when he gave in and came along, pushing the door open a few inches with his head and shoving himself through.

He walked indifferently across the room and sat by the closet door washing his shoulder for a few minutes, just to let me know he hadn't come in on account of me asking him to. Then, when he figured I'd learned my lesson, he yawned and made his way lazily to the bed. He jumped up and walked over without looking at me once.

Still, it only took a little patting and face-scratching before he started purring and snuggled in beside me.

As tired as I was, I fell asleep quickly that night. Thankfully, it was a dreamless sleep, and when I woke the next morning I felt a tiny bit better.

CHAPTER TWENTY

The next six days kind of ran together in a jumble of suffering, though there were a few things that stood out. The comments and questions at school faded after a day or two, but that was the least of it for me.

It felt like Greg was everywhere! Of course, it was normal that he'd be in the cafeteria at lunch, but I seemed to pass him in the hallways between classes way more often than I used to, and every time I caught a glimpse of him my stomach contracted with pain and I felt as though the breath had been knocked out of me.

Book club was the worst. I'd toyed with the idea of dropping out, but I didn't want to take the chance that the stalker would read that for what it was — a sign that I still really cared for Greg. What other reason would I have for avoiding him?

Pretending that everything was okay was hard enough when Greg wasn't around, but when the book club met I was forced to spend two hours in that small group — with Greg.

If he'd ignored me or even glared at me, it might have been easier, but he did neither. He didn't speak, but if we came face to face, he nodded politely the way you might do with someone you barely knew. His eyes were the worst, though: void of any emotion. It was like looking at someone in a trance.

I made an unexpected discovery in the book club meeting, too. When I first got to the room where the club met I took a seat between Annie and Sharon. To my surprise, Annie reached over and patted my hand.

"It doesn't *always* hurt this much," she whispered, just loud enough for me to hear.

I looked sideways at her and saw a shadow of sorrow in her eyes. I knew instantly that she understood exactly how I felt. She and her ex-boyfriend, Todd, had broken up sometime during the summer after going out for close to a year, but I hadn't given any particular thought to it except to think it was too bad, since they'd seemed so happy together.

Now, with one quick glance, I saw that she had carried the same pain that was weighing so heavily on my heart. And just as clearly, I could see that it was-n't gone yet, though it might not be as intense as it had been when it was fresh.

Is that going to be me in four months, I wondered? Still walking around hiding a wound, even if it isn't as raw and painful as it is right now? That thought made me realize how sincere Annie was, reaching out past her own pain to offer me a few encouraging words.

"Thanks," I whispered back, meeting her eyes.

A ghost of a smile crossed her face and her head tilted down ever so slightly — a barely perceptible acknowledgement of my gratitude.

I forced my attention back to the group, though I couldn't bring myself to join in the general discussion about the book we were reading. I noticed that Greg remained silent, too, but when we moved on to talking about our own writing he read a few paragraphs from a story he was working on. It was about a whooping crane under a silent moon.

"Oh, Greg," Sharon said softly when he'd stopped reading. "That was beautiful."

"It was," Lynn spoke up. "It was … *haunting*."

"Is it supposed to be symbolic of anything?" Jason asked.

"It's just a story about a crane," Greg said. He closed his notebook. "Who's next?"

"I'll go," Ben said quickly. "I have a poem."

Ben *always* has poems. That's all he writes. They're in free verse and, to be honest, I really don't know whether or not they're any good. This one was something about a castle that had been deserted so that it fell into ruin. Then this guy came along on a flying horse, and when he looked at it he had magic eyes or something and it was suddenly restored because that's how he saw it.

"Very interesting," Mr. Grimes said when no one else commented.

"Yeah, it was good," Nora added after a pause. "Anyway, I have a short story. Well, just the beginning of one. Should I go next?"

Nora's piece was a love tragedy, but it was totally unconvincing. A couple of the girls said it was nice, which made Nora look a bit cross.

"It's not supposed to be *nice*," she said. "It's supposed to be *moving*."

"Yes, well," Mr. Grimes said. "Everyone takes away something different from a story." Then he told us we should probably wrap things up for the evening and it was, mercifully, over.

Drama club wasn't a joy that week, either. Jimmy teased me, Eric borrowed my favourite pen and forgot to return it, and Tina asked me how I'd feel if someone else started seeing Greg that soon after we'd broken up. The way she blushed when she asked left little doubt as to who she was hoping that "someone else" would be.

"I don't care," I said, though even the *thought* of it was like getting hit hard in the stomach.

144

"For real? You don't mind?"

"I said I don't."

"I know, but if you mind *at all* ..."

"Look, if you want to ask Greg out, you go right ahead. I really don't want to talk about it for the rest of the night," I snapped. Then I realized I'd let my emotions get the better of me: if the stalker happened to be in that group, he'd be suspicious about me snapping at her. I tried to cover by claiming I had a headache and apologizing.

Unless you've ever been through something like a stalking, there's no way you can understand how much you're affected by someone with this sort of obsession. I knew that every single thing I said and did at school could be under this creep's scrutiny. Since I still had no idea who he was, I never knew when he was watching and listening, maybe even standing beside me or talking to me.

He did make contact with me twice over that period of time. The first time was another e-mail — the third that the police were able to confirm had been sent from the school. It basically said he was glad I'd realized Greg was no good for me.

The second was a letter sent through the mail. I didn't actually see it because Mom checked the mailbox earlier in the day and when she found an envelope addressed to me in block letters, she called the police.

They took it and checked for fingerprints and then put both the letter and envelope in plastic bags.

There were no fingerprints on the letter itself, and the only ones on the envelope were from the mailman and my mom.

"This guy is being careful," Officer Mueller told me when he came by to tell us they hadn't turned up a single print from the stalker. Then he went over extra security measures we should take, and promised that patrol cars would cruise our neighbourhood as often as possible until he was caught.

"Don't assume *anyone* is safe," he cautioned me. "Now, if you're feeling up to it, I've brought a copy of the letter he sent and I'd like you to go over the text to see if anything he says means anything to you."

I took the page he held out.

Soon you will be mine. I will come for you when the time is right, when everything has been made ready.

The pathway waits for your footstep. The door opens.

When all light has been obliterated, your bridegroom will come.

I read the letter three times, trying to steady the shaking of my hand. Laying the page on the table, I turned to Mueller and shook my head.

"I don't know what he means," I said. "But it sounds like he plans to come after me."

"You're not walking anywhere by yourself, are you?"

"No. Nowhere. And everywhere I go — even at school — I have this alarm keychain my dad bought for me." I showed him how it worked and the shrill siren blared for a few seconds until I shut it off.

Mueller smiled with embarrassment at the way he'd kind of jumped a bit when the alarm first went off. "That's great. It would sure bring help in a hurry," he said.

I told myself I was prepared for anything. I even convinced myself that I wished the stalker would come after me so we could catch him and it would all be over.

I guess that's what we were all expecting by then, so it was a surprise to everyone when he made a mistake that led police right to his door.

It happened on Friday evening. Mom, Dad, and I were watching a movie we'd rented. And then the phone rang.

CHAPTER TWENTY-ONE

Ever since the night I broke up with Greg, I'd stopped avoiding the phone and instead started answering it every chance I got. There just wasn't any point in having someone else get it when I was going to have to go speak to the creep anyway, and this way there was no chance he'd hang up if I didn't answer.

On this evening, when the phone rang I looked at the call display and saw an unfamiliar number registered, but no name. Still, it was more than we'd had before.

"Hello?"

"Shelby." It was the now-familiar drawn out whisper of my name.

"Yes," I said, cutting him off before he'd finished, "it's me. What do you want?"

"You," he said. It came out in a sigh, sad and heavy, as if he was sorry to have to say it.

"Who *are* you?"

"It's almost ready," he whispered, ignoring my question.

"What is?" I asked. Mom and Dad came into the kitchen, their faces anxious and questioning. I nodded. Neither made a sound.

"Just one more thing to take care of," he said, again offering no answer to my question. "Then, I'll be seeing you."

"I'd like to see you right *now*," I said. "Why don't you come on over?"

I heard him start to laugh just before he hung up.

"Where'd the call come from?" Dad asked. He came over and put his arm around me, pulling me against him where, at least for the moment, I could feel safe.

"There was no name, just a number."

"Press star fifty-seven," Mom reminded me.

I did that and then we called the police and the phone company to make sure the information was passed on right away.

Officer Stanton arrived a little while later. "It's not great news," she said. "The call came from a payphone in the mall. We've got a couple of cars on the way, but the chance that he's still going to be there isn't great, and even if he is, they won't know how to identify him."

"Which payphone?" Dad asked, his head jerking up.

"I'm not sure. Does it matter?"

"It could, if he called from the phone across from the jewellers. There are security cameras in there."

"In which case the phone call might have been caught on tape!" Officer Stanton said. You could tell she was excited as she spoke into her radio.

I tried not to get my hopes up, since there are two locations with payphones at the mall. But just a couple of moments later, Officer Stanton learned that it *had* been the one across from the jewellery store.

"The woman who runs the jewellery store said one of the cameras definitely takes in the phones, though it's a little ways off so it's not easy to see. Still, if the perp is on tape, it's got to give us *something*. They're getting the tape right now!" she said. "This could be the break we've been hoping for!"

Mom, Dad, and I piled into our car and headed to the police station, where we only waited about fifteen minutes for an officer to come in with the tape.

"Our machine is in here," he said, leading the way to a room at the end of the hall. "We'll just start back a ways, try to catch it at the approximate time the call was made, and see what we have."

He rewound it a bit too far and we watched for a while as nothing happened other than shoppers passing by outside the store. The main focus was on the display cases, so the figures in the hallway weren't very big. I wondered if I'd even be able to identify the caller when I saw him. At the same time, my impatience was growing.

And then, there he was. And while I couldn't see his face, I recognized him immediately.

"Eric," I gasped, shocked to see that he was the one. Even though Betts had told me he liked me, and he'd been kind of obvious about it himself after I broke up with Greg, I'd never really suspected him. He just seemed so harmless. "It's Eric Green."

"You're sure?"

"Yes. He has a unique jacket. See that design? The sword crossed with a candle — that's been Eric's trademark for the last few years. He does it on a lot of his stuff with some kind of permanent marker. And see — his baseball cap has the same design on the side of it. The pattern on the hat isn't very clear on this video, but if you know what you're looking at you can see what the design is."

The officer went back and froze the picture a few times. I stared at the screen each time, as if I might be able to see something there that would explain why Eric had gone from being a perfectly nice, perfectly normal guy, to a weirdo who'd turned my life into a nightmare.

"I don't suppose you happen to know where he lives."

"I do, actually. I've been there a few times with some other kids. His place is on Gallant Drive." I described the house, a pale yellow bungalow near the corner of Waters Road.

"Okay, we'll send someone over right away. In the meantime, you folks might as well go on home. We'll let you know what happens."

We did as we'd been told, but all we did when we got home was sit at the kitchen table and wait for either a phone call or a knock on the door. No one suggested that we put back on the movie we'd been watching before the stalker's phone call, even though we'd been enjoying it.

It was Mueller who pulled into the driveway close to two hours later. I could tell he had good news, but there was still something grim in his expression. I think it bothered him to have had to arrest someone that age for something so serious.

"Well, we got him," he said. "He was already back home, pretending to be sleeping, when we got there. The jacket and hat were tossed over the back of a chair right where we could see them, too."

"Did he admit it?" I asked.

"Not for a second. Denied it all the way in to the station." Mueller shook his head in disbelief. "He's *still* denying it for all the good it'll do him. His big alibi is that he was home, all alone, fast asleep on the couch.

"Anyway, we got a search warrant. There's still a team there going through things, but before I left they'd already found a copy of the letter he sent you, and another one that he was drafting. There was some other stuff written, too, which I won't go into, but it was pretty sick."

"How long will he be locked up?" Dad asked.

"We're going to see if we can hold him over the weekend and get him in front of a judge first thing Monday. I figure he'll probably be remanded, considering. At the very least, there'll be a restraining order against him."

"Which means?"

"Well, if he came anywhere near Shelby, he'd be picked up."

"Even at school?" Mom wanted to know.

"Anywhere that he knows she'll be. But let's not worry about any of that right now. Hopefully the judge will remand him. The main thing is you know you're safe right now."

We all thanked him and my Dad asked him to be sure to thank everyone else who'd worked on the case, too. Mueller said he was just glad they'd got the guy. He wished us good luck before he left.

"Well," Mom said, "it's not really over with yet, but at least the guilty boy has been caught."

"I never would have thought Eric could do something like that," I said.

"It's always the last ones you'd suspect," Dad said. "You just remember what you've been through these past weeks, and don't be going and feeling sorry for this creep."

"I don't," I said, but I kind of did, in a way. I wondered what the other pages said and whether I'd be feeling less sympathetic if Mueller had given me the details.

"Anyway, I can finally get a decent sleep tonight! And tomorrow I can do some shopping without someone coming with me to hold my hand!"

I wanted to call Greg and tell him the news. Surely, when I explained everything, and told him how much I'd missed him, he'd understand. But I was too tired for such a heavy phone call, and decided I'd wait until the next day. Maybe I could even drop by his place on my way home from the mall. For now, I just called Betts. I *had* to tell someone, even if it was just a quick call before pleading exhaustion and saying I had to go.

As I drifted off that night, it seemed that everything was going to be okay again.

CHAPTER TWENTY-TWO

I woke the next morning to the feeling of someone plopping down on the side of my bed.

"Shelby?" I heard Betts say. "You awake?"

"No … go away," I mumbled.

"It's almost eleven o'clock!"

"No it isn't." I pulled the comforter over my head, which dislodged Ernie from his spot beside me. Seconds later I heard the plunk of his feet landing on the floor and pattering away.

"Come on, you can't waste the whole day in bed," Betts said, poking at my shoulder through the blanket.

"What? *You're* telling me this?" I grumbled. "You *never* get up early on the weekend. I've called your place in the middle of the afternoon and been told you were in bed."

"Yes, but this is your first day of freedom, remember? We have to *do* something." She tugged the cover from my face and tapped on my forehead.

I opened an eye, regretting that I'd called her with the news the night before. "So you're torturing me as part of a celebration of some sort, is that it?"

She giggled. "Good! You're awake. Your mom said I should come and get your breakfast order and she'd make it while you were showering."

"My *own mother* is in on this conspiracy?"

"'Fraid so. Sad, isn't it?"

I groaned and sat up. I made a face at Betts.

"That's attractive," she said. "Oh, in case you want blueberry pancakes for breakfast, your mom said there are blueberries in the freezer."

"She just randomly announced this to you?"

"I might have asked; I'm not sure. So, anyway, you want that?"

"Blueberry pancakes?" I said slowly. "I dunno. Mom usually makes too many. Whatever would become of the rest of them?"

Betts swatted at my arm, but I saw it coming and dodged her.

"Oh, wait!" I said. "I have an idea. *You* could help eat them."

"Okay, so that's settled," she said. "Now go get in the shower."

Fifteen minutes later I made it into the kitchen,

where Betts was happily pouring syrup on a pancake. Across from her, Dad was in the middle of one, too.

"Morning, honey," Mom said, crossing the room and hugging me. "Your breakfast is ready."

"Thanks, Mom." I sat down and poured a glass of milk, then snagged a pancake from the stack on the plate in the middle of the table.

"Hey, sunshine." Dad reached over and squeezed my arm a little before lifting another fluffy forkful to his mouth.

"Hey," I said. "You're eating late this morning."

"Brunch," he told me.

"An extra meal is more like it," Mom said, but she smiled and joined us at the table.

As we all dug into our food, I thought how ordinary it was: sitting down for a meal with my family (and Betts). And suddenly, I found my eyes filling with tears.

"Shelby?" Mom said. "Is something wrong, dear?"

I shook my head and tried to explain but I couldn't quite find the words to say how I just felt overwhelmingly thankful and happy to have my life back to normal again. How amazing it was to be able to enjoy something as simple as sharing a meal without the burden I'd been carrying around, wondering where the stalker was, what he was doing, what he was thinking, and worst of all, what he was planning.

In that flash of time, it hit me that even if Greg and

I didn't get back together, I could stand it. Over the past week there had been many moments when I thought I just couldn't take any more of the hurt, when all I wanted to do was crawl into bed and stay there. Now I knew that, with or without Greg as my boyfriend, I was going to be okay.

If you've ever had a broken heart, you know how horrible it is, and how, when it first happens, it seems impossible that anything in the world will ever really be right again. But I think that moment always comes, like it did with me, when you just *know* that somehow you *will* get through it.

Annie's words floated through my head. "It doesn't *always* hurt this much." I knew she was right, that it is possible to go on with a broken heart. I'd been acting at it, pretending nothing was wrong, for a week, and there had definitely been snatches of time where I really hadn't been consumed with the pain of the break-up.

That didn't mean I wasn't hoping with all my heart that we'd be able to fix things between us, but if we didn't, I knew I could stand it.

I'd just finished sorting out my thoughts on all of this when the phone rang. The first few seconds of the ring made me cringe inside, and I had to remind myself that it wasn't going to be a call for me from the stalker.

Mom got it and spoke quietly for a moment before

covering the mouthpiece and turning to Dad and me.

"It's Alyson Stark," she said. "She wants to do a follow-up piece now that the police have someone in custody. Kind of a thank you to everyone who tried to help by calling in anything they saw that was suspicious. What do you think?

"I don't want another problem with the police," Dad said. "They weren't exactly thrilled that we talked to her before."

"Yes, but that was just because we *could* have compromised the investigation, even though we *didn't* because we were careful about what we said to her," Mom pointed out. "And in any case, it all worked out okay and the investigation is over. I think it would be nice for us to acknowledge the help the community gave."

"Oh, I don't suppose it will hurt. Shelby, do you mind?"

"No, I don't care, but Betts and I were planning to go to the mall later. Would she be coming over soon?"

Mom went back to the phone and talked for another minute or so. After she hung up she told us that Mrs. Stark would be along shortly.

Betts and I did the dishes while we waited, me washing and her drying. We'd just finished when the knock came.

"Shelby, honey, you must be *so* relieved to have this whole thing over with," Mrs. Stark said as she whipped out a notebook and pen. "Why, when I think of my Nora being the very same age as you and I picture her going through something like this, I just shudder.

"Now, there was one thing I didn't get confirmed when I spoke to the police, and that was the identity of the stalker. It was the Green boy, wasn't it? Eric Green?"

"Did you ask the police that question?" Dad asked before I could say anything.

"Well, I, uh, I'm not sure if they're allowed to confirm that."

"Because the suspect is a minor?"

"Something like that," she said vaguely. "They don't really explain things very well sometimes. You know how it is."

"My understanding," Mom said, "is that you're not allowed to give out the name of a minor who's accused of a crime."

"Well, no," Mrs. Stark admitted. "We can't print the name."

"Then why do you need it?" Dad asked. She blushed, and stammered something unintelligible. It occurred to me that she'd just been busted digging for gossip instead of actual news.

"Maybe we can just go ahead and talk about the things you *can* print," Mom suggested.

Mrs. Stark recovered from her embarrassment with amazing speed. She brightened right up and launched into some quick questions about our reaction to the news that a suspect had been apprehended. Then she got a "thank you" statement from us and wrapped it up. The whole thing probably didn't take more than five minutes.

Mom and Dad saw her to the door, but after they'd said goodbye, Dad turned with a kind of disgusted look on his face.

"That was nothing more than a fishing expedition," he said. "Abusing her position, trying to get information she's really not entitled to. I wouldn't be in a hurry to talk to her again."

Mom agreed, though she added that maybe they should give her the benefit of a doubt and that it's probably just in Mrs. Stark's nature to ask questions and dig for information, because of her job.

If Betts thought anything about that, or realized that gossipers aren't always viewed kindly, she sure didn't mention it to me. Her mind was on going to the mall … and one other thing.

"Did I tell you that the party at Tyrone's place was changed to tonight?" she asked. (She *had* told me — about twenty times.) "Now that you're single again, you should go."

"I don't think so."

"Why not? Is it in case … oh, never mind."

"In case what?"

"You know, in case Greg is there. With Tina."

CHAPTER TWENTY-THREE

I stared at Betts, hardly able to believe that she'd just *casually* told me that Greg might be going to Tyrone's party with Tina. How could she not realize that it would hurt me to hear something like that?

I reminded myself that I'd been acting as if I'd *wanted* the break-up, so there'd be no reason for Betts to think I'd care if Greg was already seeing someone else.

And, really, *that* was what was so shocking to me: the idea that he'd found a new girlfriend so quickly. It was as if I'd meant nothing to him.

That would have been the time to come clean with Betts, to tell her the truth about the whole thing, but pride held me back.

So, just like I'd been doing ever since I broke up with Greg, I swallowed it all down and forced myself to smile. And then I said the dumbest thing I'd said in a long time.

"I don't care if Greg is there with *ten* other girls. In fact, I think I *will* go to the party."

Betts squealed and hugged me and didn't seem to notice that I was blinking faster than normal, or that my smile was phoney and frozen in place.

"This is great!" she said. "Maybe we'll *both* get new boyfriends tonight. That would be cool."

I thought it would be anything but cool. I also thought she was kind of getting a bit ahead of herself as far as Kevin was concerned, but I didn't say either of those things. To be honest, I wasn't sure I could speak properly just then.

"Anyway, let's hurry up and get ready to go shopping. I want to look for something new to wear tonight." Betts was shifting into high gear — her normal speed when there's shopping involved. "Hey! You should too!"

Buying new clothes was the last thing on my mind. The only reason I'd wanted to go to the mall at all was to try to finish my Christmas shopping. I'd even thought maybe I'd find something just right for Greg, that's how sure I'd been that we'd make up.

While I got ready to head out, I wondered what on earth had made me decide to go to Tyrone's party. It was like I was drawn to it against my will, as if a magnetic force was making me go. It really didn't make any sense. And yet, I knew I wasn't going to back out, no matter how awful it might feel to be at a party with Greg — not as his girlfriend, but as his ex — while he danced and laughed with someone else.

You did this to me, I thought, picturing Eric's face. I never did a single thing to you, but you started this whole thing and scared me and forced me to do this.

In that moment, the most powerful anger I could ever remember feeling filled me to the point that I was actually shaking. I wanted to scream until my throat was raw, to throw things until exhaustion overtook me. Mostly, I wanted to make Eric Green suffer for what he'd done.

What I did instead was take some deep breaths and join Betts in the kitchen. Mom glanced up from some pictures she had spread over the table.

"Shelby?"

"Yeah?"

"Are you all right, dear?"

"Fine," I said. You can fool a lot of people, but it's almost impossible to fool your mother! "I, uh, have a bit of a headache, but I'm sure it'll pass when I get some fresh air."

"You're sure?" She neither looked nor sounded convinced, but I knew she wouldn't push it with Betts there.

"Yup. Anyway, we have to go."

"Well, have a good time. Oh! Just a sec. Betts tells me you two are looking for something to wear to a party this evening."

"Uh, maybe."

"Here's something to put toward it." She dug into her wallet and passed me a couple of twenties.

"Thanks, Mom." I took the money and stuck it into my purse, knowing I'd just give it back later.

Betts and I started toward the mall and I have to admit that it was nice to be able to walk along the streets of Little River without wondering and worrying about being stalked. We window-shopped as we passed through town, making note of any stores we might want to check out later on.

The mall is only about a twenty-minute walk from my place, but it took us almost twice that to get there. When we did, Betts tried to talk me into trying on clothes with her, but I insisted I had to get my shopping finished. We split up and I promised to meet her at Francine's Boutique a bit later on.

I'd already bought things for Mom and Dad and all of my grandparents, as well as a couple of cat toys with catnip in them for Ernie. It's a habit of mine to finish all of the family members first, and then buy for anyone else on my list. This year there had only been Betts, Greg, and Mr. Stanley, but, as you know, Greg was no longer on the list.

It didn't take long to find just the right thing for Betts. She loves earrings for special occasions, and as soon as I saw a pair with a snowman couple (I guess that would actually be one snowman, and one *snow-woman*) I knew it would be perfect for her.

Mr. Stanley was a little harder, but I finally decided on a big, fluffy pair of slippers that were made to look like bear paws. I remembered him mentioning that the nursing home was a nice place, but they never had the heat high enough to suit him and his feet would get cold a lot.

I was on my way back to where Betts was (her gift hidden away in my purse) when a pretty satin lipstick holder caught my attention in a store that mainly sells purses, hats, and gloves. It was pale blue with two tiny daffodils crossed over each other on the front — a design that kind of stood out amid all the red and green holiday stuff.

On impulse, I bought it for Annie Berkley. We'd never been close friends or anything, and she's a very shy person, so her kindness the other day had really meant something to me. I'd just write her a note on a card telling her so, and wish her a happy Christmas on the last day of school before the holidays.

"Hey, Shelby!"

I turned to see Ben Hebert and Jimmy Farrell hurrying toward me.

"Hi you guys."

"That is *so* freaky about Eric," Jimmy said. "What do you think will happen to him?"

"I have no idea, really," I felt uncomfortable talking about it, but didn't want to be rude either. "And, uh, I was just on my way …"

"He'll probably get sent to the nuthouse," Ben interrupted. "Anyone who'd do something that weird should be locked up, don't you think?"

"Well, he needs help, for sure," I said, wishing I hadn't been drawn into the conversation at all.

"I always thought he was a bit strange," Ben said. I expected I'd be hearing a lot of that over the coming weeks.

"I really have to …"

"Hey!" Ben interrupted for the second time. "We just saw Betts and she told us you guys are going to the party at Tyrone's place tonight. It should be pretty cool. Everyone's going to be there."

"Okay, then …"

"Yeah, so I'll see you there," Jimmy said. He looked embarrassed.

"Uh, okay, see you later." I gave a wave, even though I was standing right beside them, and walked away as quickly as I could.

I got to Francine's Boutique just as Betts was coming out of the dressing room with her arms full of clothes. She sorted through them, kept two pairs of pants and three tops, marched to the cash register, and passed the salesgirl a credit card.

"I can't decide," she said innocently, "but I need some new things anyway. You gonna try some things on here?"

"I can't," I said, and added, before she could protest, "I need to go home and lie down for a while."

"Oh. Well, that's too bad. Do you want me to go with you?"

"No, you stay and shop or whatever. I'll talk to you later and we can make plans."

"All right." Betts came over and gave me a quick hug. "Feel better, okay?"

"I'll be fine. I just need to rest for a bit. Have fun shopping."

I headed toward the nearest exit, passing the phone where Eric had made the call that tripped him up. Something made me stop and stare at it for a minute, as if it could explain why a kid who seemed perfectly normal would flip out that way. Then I hurried out the door and made it home in record time.

Mr. Stanley was there, having a chat with my dad and, of course, stroking Ernie. Forgetting about lying down, I joined them for a while and then helped Mom get dinner on the table. When I called the men to come and eat, Dad helped Mr. Stanley up. He looked small and frail next to my father.

As if he'd read my mind, he smiled over at me. "They say you get shorter when you get older. It's true too," he

168

said, gesturing to a picture on the wall behind him. "There was a time if I'd been standing in front of this picture, you wouldn't have seen it at all. Now, you can see pretty near the whole thing." His eyes twinkled then and he added, "Why, would you believe I used to be six-one?"

I giggled at that. Mr. Stanley is only an inch or two taller than me, though it's hard to tell because of his stoop.

"Okay, maybe it was five-seven. Can't a feller claim a few inches in his old age?"

"Sure you can." I pulled his chair out and Dad helped him settle into it. Mom asked him if he'd like to say the blessing, like she does every time he visits.

"Heavenly Father," he intoned, "thank you very much for these good people and the food we're going to share, and for watching over this little girl here, who we all love. Amen."

My eyes were moist as I opened them and started passing around the food. In no time, though, I was listening to Mr. Stanley's stories, just like my folks were.

CHAPTER TWENTY-FOUR

Betts and I had just started out walking toward Tyrone's place, which is on the outskirts of town and a good half hour away, when we heard a car horn. We turned toward the sound in time to hear someone call my name.

"Shelby! I thought that was you." As the window came down I saw that it was Webster.

"Oh, hello," I answered. I felt immediately uncomfortable, remembering how he'd acted at the last book club meeting he'd attended. I also got thinking about what Jimmy and Sheri had overheard Grimes saying about him not taking his medications. But the real discomfort hit when I remembered that he'd been questioned as my potential stalker. What must he think of me?

"Kind of a cold night for you girls to be out walking," he said. His voice sounded calm and normal.

"I know! And we're going all the way to Standover Ridge," Betts chimed in. "We'll be frozen by the time we get there."

It really *wasn't* that cold out and I could see what Betts was up to, but I was powerless to do anything about it. The next thing I knew, Webster was saying he was going that way and offering us a drive. Betts was in the car in a flash and I reluctantly got in beside her. I wondered how she could just jump into a car with someone she'd never met before, just because he happened to know my name.

I'm probably only hearing alarm bells because of the stalker thing, I thought. On the other hand, even before that whole business, I'd always been more cautious than Betts.

Five minutes later, when we were getting out of Webster's car and thanking him for the drive, I felt a little silly. He'd been perfectly fine, chatting with us about school and the usual stuff adults talk about with teens. I figured he must be taking his pills again.

We knocked at the front door of Tyrone's place but no one came. It wasn't hard to figure out why.

"They can't hear us," Betts said, turning the door-knob. It wasn't locked, so she just pushed the door open and we went in.

The music was as loud as you'd expect, which made conversation a bit of a problem. This wasn't stopping anyone there, as far as I could tell. There were a lot of voices talking over the song that was playing in the downstairs rec room, which is where Betts and I made our way.

I saw them as soon as we walked into the room: Greg and Tina. He was sitting on the couch, and she was perched beside him on the arm, smiling down at him in a way that left no doubt about how happy she was to be there with him.

At my side, I felt Betts stiffen and look at me. I knew she'd seen them too, and was watching for my reaction. I let my gaze drift around the room, doing my best to act as though there wasn't a horrible ache swelling inside me.

He saw me. I sensed this even though I didn't actually see him look over. I told myself that whatever I did, I must *not* let him know I cared. And then, to my horror, I saw him coming toward me as the song playing on the surround-sound ended.

"Hi," he said.

"Oh, hi."

"How are you?"

"Me? I'm fine. You?" Like that wasn't obvious, since he was there with Tina.

"Okay. Anyway, I heard they got him. The stalker, I mean. Eric."

"Yeah."

"I'm really glad for you."

"Thanks." The opening riffs of another song filled the air around us. It was a slow song, and it was all I could do not to reach out for him. I could hardly breathe.

He stood there for what seemed a long time, but was probably less than a minute. It looked like he was trying to think of something else to say, but in the end he just turned and walked away. He didn't go back to the couch, but joined a group of kids who were looking at the CDs. Tina was at his side in a flash, like she needed to make sure everyone realized they were a couple.

"Dance?" Through blurring vision I saw that the invitation came from Jimmy Roth, who seemed to have appeared from nowhere.

"Thanks but, uh ... maybe later, Jimmy."

"You look upset."

"No, I'm fine."

"What's the problem?" His voice had turned mocking and I realized that he'd been drinking. "You change your mind about Greg now that someone else has him?"

"Hey, Jimmy, ease up, man." Jason Puckett, who'd been standing somewhere to my left, stepped forward.

Jimmy mumbled something but backed away quickly, which was no surprise, considering that Jason is a fair bit taller and stronger than him.

"Thanks, Jason."

"No problem. It's kind of hard to enjoy a party with someone bothering you like that."

"I guess." I could have told him that I wasn't exactly enjoying the party, but instead I gave him a weak smile and went in search of Betts. I found her, as expected, talking to Kevin Montoya, her eyes shining as she looked up at him.

"I'm going to head home," I told her, leaning down near her ear. "It wasn't a good idea for me to come."

She nodded to show that she understood, offered to leave with me, and looked relieved when I told her not to be silly, to stay and have a good time.

I retrieved my coat and left, walking briskly along the street. Before I reached the first corner, I heard footsteps running toward me.

"Sorry if I startled you," Jason said, falling in beside me. "I heard Jimmy say something about teaching you a lesson or whatever, so I thought maybe it would be good if someone walked you home."

"Thanks," I said, "but I'm sure I'll be fine. I hate to see you miss the party."

"The party was a drag anyway."

I wanted to tell him that I'd really rather be alone, but that seemed rude when he'd just come to my rescue with Jimmy, and was trying to be nice and look out for me. So I managed a smile and didn't object any further.

We walked in silence for a few minutes and then, as we neared the street that led downtown, he asked if I knew about the route through the old campground. It was on private land, but it had closed a few years back when the old couple who used to run it didn't want to be bothered anymore.

"It's actually a shortcut if you know the right path," Jason said.

"Too much snow," I said. "I'm not wearing boots."

He didn't argue, but something about the suggestion bothered me. I couldn't picture how it would be shorter to go that way and I was pretty familiar with the area, since it bordered a part of the woods Greg and I used to explore a lot.

We turned the corner and I noticed for the first time that he was wearing some kind of cologne or aftershave. It seemed vaguely familiar, though I was sure it wasn't like anything my dad or Greg had ever worn. I'd never smelled anything like that on Jason at school either, so I figured he probably just put it on if he was going somewhere special. Lots of guys do that.

We'd only walked a few minutes along the street that would take us into town when for some reason I thought of Mr. Stanley and his comment about getting shorter.

"*There was a time if I'd been standing in front of this picture, you wouldn't have seen it at all,*" he'd said. "*Now, you can see pretty near the whole thing.*"

I wondered why that would come to mind now, and why it seemed to be bothering me.

When the significance of his remark hit me, everything else tumbled into place with lightning speed.

Eric Green wasn't the stalker at all. The stalker was walking at my side.

CHAPTER TWENTY-FIVE

Maybe if I'd remained calm and just kept walking, if I'd managed to act as if everything was okay, I'd have made it home that night. But fear clutched me so tightly I could hardly breathe, and the only thought that made any sense was ... run!

That's exactly what I did. I took off, racing down the street as fast as I could go. But I hadn't made it ten feet when I heard him coming after me, his footsteps pounding as he, too, broke into a run. My heart was thudding so hard I thought it would explode as I heard him get closer and closer.

Before I'd reached the end of the street I felt his hand grab my arm and yank it. I started to scream, but he spun me around and pulled me against him so fast that the wind was knocked out of me.

His hand clamped over my mouth and he leaned

down, staring into my eyes. "You disappoint me, Shelby," he said, almost chewing his words through clenched teeth. "So I see we're going to do this the hard way. Now, are you going to try to scream?"

I shook my head "no," forcing myself to meet his eyes. The second he started to move his hand away I bit it as hard as I could, stomping on his foot at the same time. With every bit of strength I could muster, I broke away and started to run again. As I ran, I tried to get a deep enough breath to be able to scream, but I needed every bit of oxygen to keep going.

Around the corner! Just ahead was a bungalow. If I could make it there, someone would help me. And then I felt something grab my ankles and I went down. I knew he had to have thrown himself down, too, in order to get a hold of me and pull me off my feet, so I kicked behind me, freeing my legs.

Frantically, I crawled forward, ploughing through snow on the lawn as I tried to get closer to the house. I managed to yell "help," but I doubted it was loud enough to attract attention. Too late, I remembered my alarm keychain. I had just begun to reach for it when — *wham*! — I was down again, my face buried in the snow and the weight of Jason crushing me to the ground.

I struggled, my lungs exploding with the need for air while my face remained pressed in the snow. I felt as though I was fighting so hard to free myself, but even as blackness closed in I knew my efforts were feeble and futile.

I have no idea how long I was unconscious. All I know is that when I woke up, I was in a different place — a dark place that smelled musty and stale. My hands and feet were tied and there was some kind of wide tape across my mouth. I didn't move or make a sound while I waited for my eyes to adjust enough for me to get some idea of where I was.

Light from the moon, shining through a solitary window, soon made it possible for me to see that I was in a small building — a shed, maybe. It was clear from the window's position, not to mention the hard surface underneath me, that I was lying on the floor.

There were a couple of stools along with a folding table off to one side, and as far as I could see they were the only pieces of furniture in here. There was no sign of Jason, and I was pretty sure he wasn't somewhere behind me, but I waited and listened carefully just in case. When enough time had passed without the slightest sound — no breathing, no shifting around, nothing — I decided I was, indeed, alone.

Now that I knew it was *safe* to move, I was left with the question of whether or not I *could* move. Thankfully, my hands were tied in front of me and not behind, which would have made movement much more difficult. A third rope ran from the cords on my wrists through the belt loops on my jeans, making it impossible for me to lift my hands up more than a few inches. I assumed this was mainly to keep me from removing the tape that covered my mouth. I managed to get into a sitting position after trying a few times, but I could see standing up was going to be a lot more difficult. Even so, I made a couple of attempts, both of which landed me flat on the floor and back where I started.

I need to get to that window, I thought, to see where I am. The campground? Maybe that's why Jason wanted to take the "shortcut."

Then I realized the problem with getting to my feet was balance. I got into a kneeling position and inched my way over to the closest stool. With something to put my hands on to steady myself, I managed to get upright.

The window was only a few feet away, but there was so little movement possible with my ankles tied that it seemed to take forever to get there. As I shuffled along, my heart began to pound in fright. What if he came back before I got to the window? I knew if that happened he'd make sure I never had another chance.

It was odd, really, how my thoughts were all focused entirely on seeing out that window. Not on escaping or getting help, but just on knowing where I was. I guess I knew that if I tried to think of too many things at once, it would seem hopeless and I'd become overwhelmed. Setting one, simple goal and working on that helped me stay clear-headed.

Once I found out where I was, I could think of the next step. Not before. And so I put every bit of concentration into getting to that window, listening all the while for any sounds of someone approaching.

When at last I reached it I saw that I was, as I'd suspected, in a building on the abandoned campground. I was quite sure it was a little shed that had been used for storage, one that wasn't close enough to the owner's home for any noise to reach them.

The nearest street was the one I'd been on when I'd started running, and there were no houses on it at all. All it did was connect Cedar Street, where Jason had caught me, and Standover Ridge Road, where Tyrone's house was. I couldn't picture any houses near enough that the inhabitants would be able hear me. Or, I should say, to hear the alarm Dad had bought me.

And the light on the alarm wasn't bright enough to attract attention, either. I touched the keychain anyway, to reassure myself that Jason hadn't realized what it was and taken it. It was still there, hanging from my coat zipper, but as my fingers closed around it I knew immediately that something was wrong.

It felt too light, for one thing, and a quick exploration with my fingers told me that the little plastic flap that closed over the batteries was missing. And so were the batteries. At first I thought Jason had taken them, but when I managed to turn the alarm around to look at it, I could see there was a chip near where the flap had been, and a crack near it. Obviously, it had busted open and the batteries had fallen out one of the times Jason had hurled me to the ground.

I almost started to cry. Everything in me wanted to give in to that urge to sink back onto the floor and weep with despair. To give up.

I might have surrendered to the urge, too, even for a few moments, except I pictured Mom and Dad, how frantic they'd be when I didn't come home from the party. And I knew I had to do every last thing in my power to get out of that shed. That meant not wasting even a moment on self-pity, and it meant not giving up for one single second.

I wondered then for the first time if they realized yet that I was missing. I had no watch on and no idea what time it was. It could have been an hour since I'd left the party; it could have been six.

Someone will come looking for me, I thought. I wondered about footprints, but it had been weeks since we'd had a snowfall and there were always people going through the old campground to the trails in the woods. Besides, even if someone noticed a set of footprints coming up to the shed, there'd be no reason to tie me to them. Since Jason must have carried me, there'd just be one set of prints: his.

I made my way to the door, repeating the slow, shuffling walk that had taken me to the window. I knew there was no way Jason had just left me there with the door unsecured, but I had to check, just in case.

It was locked, as I'd expected. The handle turned okay, but the door itself only budged a fraction of an inch when I pushed and pulled on it. I figured there was a padlock on the outside.

I tried throwing myself against the door in the hope that some of the wood would be old enough to give, but all I managed to do was fall over from the attempt.

Back on my knees, back to the stool, back onto my feet. It was frustrating to have something as simple as standing up take so long because of the ropes. This time I'd no sooner gotten to my feet than I heard sounds outside.

I felt my pulse quicken again as footsteps drew closer. Please let it be someone looking for me, I begged silently, but when I heard a key in the lock, I knew it was Jason.

I almost dropped back to the floor to make him think I'd been lying there the whole time. I started to bend my knees, then I hesitated and straightened back up. He might be holding me captive, but at least I could be standing when I faced him. It was the closest I could come to defying him, to showing any strength at all.

And that was how he found me when the door swung open and he stepped inside.

CHAPTER TWENTY-SIX

Jason stopped in surprise when he saw me standing and staring at him. Recovering quickly, he smiled — a wide, friendly smile that scared me more than a scowl would have. Without taking his gaze off of me, he set a plastic bag he was carrying on the floor beside the door. I could see that it was full, but I couldn't tell what was in it.

"So, you're awake," he said.

I frowned at him and pointed my thumbs up to the tape covering my mouth.

"Oh, yeah." He crossed the small room until he was standing right in front of me. "Sorry about that, but you can appreciate that I couldn't exactly trust you without it. Not after you tried to run away."

He reached up and stroked my hair, pushing it back from my face. I somehow managed to keep from flinching at his touch. Then he took hold of the edge of the tape and peeled it off as slowly and painlessly as possible.

"You understand if you scream — not that anyone can hear you way out here — but if you do, the tape will go back on to stay."

"Yes." After the violent way he'd slammed me to the ground earlier, I was surprised at how calm and gentle he seemed. I forced myself to look at him and almost shivered involuntarily when I met his eyes.

He's insane, I thought, fighting panic. The eyes that looked back at me had a strangely vacant wildness to them. I knew with absolute certainty that there would be no reasoning with him. Jason was clearly living in a fantasy of his own creation.

"You know, Jason, someone is going to come looking for me," I said. I didn't really think there was much chance that he'd move me somewhere else, but I hoped at least to shake him up, get him worried.

"They probably will, but not tonight," he said. His hand touched my face, caressed it. It was all I could do not to flinch.

"Tonight won't last much longer," I said. I kept my voice from wavering but couldn't ignore the fact that his total unconcern could mean that his plans didn't extend past this one night.

"No need for you to worry about it, my love." He leaned forward and kissed my cheek. Again, I kept

186

myself from reacting, though ever fibre in my body wanted to recoil. "I have everything under control. No one will find you here. You're safe with me."

I felt my throat tighten as I realized that, in Jason's mind, I didn't *want* to be found. I was there willingly — gladly, even. In order to go on with the fantasy that we were destined for each other, he'd persuaded himself that I cared for him.

I wondered if he was actually delusional enough to believe that his feelings were reciprocated. If I could convince him that his fantasy had any truth to it, it might be possible for me to somehow trick him into letting me go.

"Oh, I brought you some food and water," he said, pointing to the bag he'd put on the floor when he first came in. He went to the bag and drew out a couple of bottles of water, some sandwiches, and three tangerines.

"You want a drink of water?"

"Maybe a little," I said with a shrug. In fact, I was desperately thirsty. My throat felt dry and parched, but I didn't want him to think he was doing anything nice for me. If he wanted to "win my affection," he'd be doing it on my terms, not his. It was the single area in which I might have the slightest control and I had to turn it to my advantage. But I had to do it in such a way that he still felt the power was all his.

Jason held a bottle to my lips so that I could drink. I took a few good swallows and then pretended to choke.

"Oh, sorry," he said, putting the bottle down and patting my back.

"You did the best you could," I said, still coughing between words. "It's hard to give someone else a drink without choking them."

He didn't say anything to that, but I could tell he was thinking about it. Don't ask him directly for anything, I told myself. Just plant the ideas and let him decide. I have to make sure he feels in charge at all times.

What was it that Dr. Taylor had said? Oh, yes. "He thrives on the sense of power he's created for himself."

"You hungry?"

"Not really. Thanks." I kept my voice respectful, but not particularly grateful. "I, uh, need to use the bathroom, Jason."

"No problem. I have everything figured out." He smiled and pointed to a corner and I saw for the first time that there was a small pail there. "I even brought some toilet paper."

I couldn't speak for a few seconds. When I did, I was unable to keep my voice steady. "You're going to untie my hands so I can do this myself, right?"

"Maybe." He smiled and the nice guy seemed to vanish. "But first, you have to tell me something."

"Sure. What?"

"How'd you figure it out?"

"That it was you and not Eric?" I thought about what to tell him and decided on a mixture of the truth and a few things that might help me.

"Well, for one thing, Eric seemed, you know, *wrong*," I said. "I couldn't picture him being smart or brave enough to be the one."

Jason's eyes narrowed slightly. I decided I might be laying it on a bit too thick. "But the first thing that really told me it was you was your cologne. I recognized the scent when we turned the corner and I caught the first whiff of it, only it took me a minute to figure out when I'd smelled it before.

"It's funny how your brain works, don't you think?" I went on, trying to make it all sound normal, like we were just chatting about some ordinary thing. "The scent triggered thoughts of Mr. Stanley. He's a friend of our family, and our cat's former owner. And I remembered a comment Mr. Stanley had made about his height, and how there was a time he'd have been tall enough to block out a picture on the wall, but he wasn't anymore."

"So?" Jason looked impatient.

"So, that made me think about the video of the phone call that Eric supposedly made from the mall. It had seemed like an awfully careless mistake for someone to make after being so clever up until then. And it was Mr. Stanley's remark about height that made me realize it wasn't a mistake at all. It was deliberate — and done to frame Eric.

"You're a good four or five inches taller than Eric, but he's not much taller than me. The person on the video blocked out the whole phone, but Eric couldn't have done that. He's not tall enough."

Jason looked anything but pleased and I knew he was probably thinking that the police might stop and look more carefully at the evidence against Eric now that I'd disappeared.

"How'd you get his jacket and hat, anyway?" I asked, doing my best to sound worried. "They can't tie you to it, can they?"

"No way," he said, but I could see he was trying to convince himself as much as me. "A bunch of us went skating at the rink after school on Friday. I bought everyone a hot chocolate after we were done ... only Eric's had a little something extra in it. Something to, let's say, *relax* him. His parents both work evenings, so once he was asleep it was nothing to go into his house, get his jacket, and plant the other evidence."

"So you went to the mall and made the phone call knowing you had lots of time to take the hat and jacket back to Eric's before the police could check out the surveillance tape and get to his place." I hoped I sounded admiring, and I must have been convincing because Jason smiled proudly.

"It would have been foolproof, except for the height thing. I never thought of anyone noticing that." He frowned then. "But, you said there was something else. My cologne?"

"Yes. Once I'd realized the part about the height, I remembered where I'd smelled that cologne before. It was on my cat a couple of weeks ago when Mr. Stanley was visiting. And I realized that was why it had taken me so long to find him, and why he didn't come when I called him. You were hiding somewhere outside my place, weren't you? Behind some bushes or a hedge."

Jason put his head back and laughed out loud. "You're right," he said once he'd stopped. "That stupid cat came along sniffing at me just as you started calling him. I was afraid he'd give me away, so I just picked him up and held him until you were gone down the street."

He looked at me and shook his head admiringly. "Well, Shelby, my love, I'd say we're a well-matched pair. What do you think?"

"I think I'd like to be able to go to the bathroom in privacy," I said. I hoped I wasn't pushing it, and apparently I wasn't.

Jason unfastened the ropes holding my wrists together and led me over to the corner where the bucket stood.

"I'll turn my back and stand over by the door," he

said. "But if you try anything, it will be the last time your hands are free. Got it?"

"Got it," I said.

CHAPTER TWENTY-SEVEN

"Well, I'd better get going before someone at home gets up and notices I'm not there," Jason said, yawning and standing up. He'd been seated across from me on one of the stools for what seemed like hours, mainly telling me how clever he'd been.

Most of what he'd said was just empty bragging, but I'd listened carefully, picking out the bits of information that might be useful to me. Some of what I'd heard was discouraging, even though it was good for me to know.

Like the fact that Jason had gone back to the party at Tyrone's place after he'd tied me and left me in the shed.

"Far as anyone there knows, I never left," he laughed. "If you ever need an alibi, a crowded party is perfect. Someone sees you at nine-thirty and again at eleven, there's no reason for them to think you ever left.

Not with so many kids moving around from one room to another, or hanging outside."

"What if someone was looking specifically for you?" I asked, feigning concern for him.

"I had a story to cover that," he smirked, "but it never came up. I went through the whole place a few times to make sure everyone saw me. If anyone had been looking for me while I was gone they'd have said so."

"What if I hadn't gone to the party?" How I wished I hadn't!

"I didn't even know you'd be there," he said. "I just knew that once I framed someone else, you'd drop the bodyguard thing and go places on your own again. Knowing that we're meant to be together, I was sure you'd find your way to me sooner or later."

Find my way to him? Maybe in Jason's warped thinking, I'd just waltzed right into the shed on my own and tied myself up. It was hard to keep from glaring at him, or telling him he was crazy.

It also took tremendous willpower not to ask him what he planned to do with me. You can imagine the kinds of things that went through my head, though, and it was all I could do not to let those thoughts show on my face as we talked.

And now it was nearing dawn and he apparently planned to leave me there and go home. He'd left my hands untied while we'd talked, but my ankles were still bound and I knew he wouldn't be leaving me with my hands loose.

All I kept thinking was that, first thing in the morning, there'd be a search party out looking for me. Since the campground was fairly close to Tyrone's place, where I'd last been seen, it was practically guaranteed that people would look there. All I'd have to do would be to stand by the window and wait. If necessary, I could bang my head against the glass to make sure someone noticed me.

"I wish you hadn't run," he said sadly, coming to stand in front of me. "It makes it impossible for me to trust you, you know."

"I'm sorry."

He didn't respond to my apology, but he smiled when I held my hands up for him to tie. Resisting would only get me hurt, and the more compliant I seemed the less suspicious he'd be that I'd try to get away.

It was only after my hands were tightly bound and connected to my waist, and after a fresh piece of heavy duct tape covered my mouth, that Jason revealed the horror he had in store for me. I should have been suspicious when he emptied the bucket that had served as my toilet into an old ice cream container, and stuck the bucket up in the rafters, where you'd never notice it unless you were actually looking for it.

That alone should have alerted me. I mean, if he took the time to hide a bucket, he wasn't about to leave me in plain view.

What a fool I'd been to believe for one moment that he wouldn't have thought through every possibility. Of course he knew people would be coming around!

"This is unfortunate, but necessary, I'm afraid," he said as he moved the stools and table out of place. I watched in shock as he lifted out some of the floor-boards, revealing a space between the crossbeams. I could see nothing past that, but I knew immediately that he meant to put me down in that dark hole.

I would have given in then, screamed and begged, if only I could have spoken. With my mouth taped, all I could do was turn pleading eyes toward him and shake my head frantically.

"It's just for a while, my love," he said, his voice calm and matter-of-fact. "And don't worry. I've made it as comfortable down there as it can be, under the circumstances. It's not ideal, but you'll be warm enough, and, more importantly, safe from prying eyes."

Every part of me screamed against what was happening, and yet I was helpless to prevent it. Lifting me like I was a rag doll, Jason lowered me through the opening onto a blanket that was already stretched out and waiting. Tears were running from my eyes as he reached down and slid a heavy nylon cord through the ties on my wrists. I saw that it was lashed to one of the beams, and would keep me from moving around under the building.

Finally, he covered me with a couple of blankets and told me he'd be back later, when it was "safe." Then the floorboards were laid back in place, and darkness closed in.

I heard Jason move the table and stools back to their original positions. I heard the shed door creak open and then close again. I heard footsteps go down a couple of stairs, followed by a sort of whishing sound I couldn't identify. And then there was silence.

I'd never before experienced that kind of darkness. It was so black down there that the air almost seemed solid, and at first it was a terrible struggle to breathe. But as I writhed and strained for air I realized that the blankets Jason had placed over me were beginning to shift.

It wasn't as cold as it can be this time of year, but it was still cold enough that death from exposure was an immediate risk. Almost immobile from the ties and lack of space, my only chance to keep from freezing was if I stayed under those blankets. And if I knocked them off myself, I had no way of getting them back in place.

Those thoughts forced me to calm down, to focus on taking even breaths. I told myself over and over that I was okay, that this was just for a little while. There's no shortage of air, I reminded myself. It's dark and confined, but there's no actual danger, and I won't be here for long.

That was the thing, though. I didn't know how long I'd be there. What if Jason never came back? What if he thought someone suspected him? What if he thought he was being followed? If something made him nervous, he might be afraid to come back.

Don't think about things like that! I told myself sternly, but keeping negativity out of my head wasn't easy. Even so, I did my best to concentrate on other thoughts. Song lyrics, happy memories ... anything that would keep me from panicking.

Mercifully, exhaustion overtook me at some point and I fell asleep. When I woke up later on I had to fight down all the fears and other thoughts and feelings again. After a bit, I saw that it was a little lighter in my dirt prison, so I knew it was daylight outside. Even the tiny bits of light that seeped in through the building's boards helped.

I wondered what time it was, and whether a search party had been organized yet. News of this sort would travel fast in Little River, so it was possible searchers had set out at the first sign of dawn.

I listened hard, straining for any sound that might mean someone was approaching. If anyone came into the cabin I'd risk losing my blankets by trying to kick the floor, though I knew from making tentative movements earlier that there was very little space in which I could gain any momentum. Even so, a single thud would save me.

The first sounds I heard weren't searchers, though. Rather, a scratching, scurrying noise somewhere in the area of my left foot made me aware that I wasn't alone down there after all.

It's only mice, I told myself, but images of rats pushed through anyway. Pictures of their beady eyes and horrid faces rose in my head, followed immediately by thoughts brought on by every horror story I'd ever heard about rats. I had to fight hard against fears of being crawled over and chewed on. I knew that I couldn't give in to them, that these fears would destroy the calm I'd struggled so hard to win.

There was nothing I could do but wait to see if whatever was making the scuffling sounds came near enough to my face for me to make out its size. And, to be perfectly honest, I wasn't at all anxious to see it, if it was, indeed, a rat.

I was putting so much concentration into these thoughts — and working so hard on staying calm — that I didn't hear the searchers at first.

The first sound to penetrate was that of my name being called over and over. Different voices calling out, some of them getting closer and closer. They're doing a grid search, I thought. Someone will check this building!

And they did. I heard feet come up the steps and rattle the door. I heard them call, "Shelby?" I heard voices by the window and envisioned them looking in, shining a light around, seeing only an empty shed.

I banged my feet on the beam, disgusted with how insignificant and muffled the sound was. I made the loudest "Mmm" sound I could, but even as I did I knew it wasn't carrying outside. They might have heard it if they were standing right over top of me, but without coming inside there wasn't a prayer.

The last thing I heard distinctly was a man's voice saying, "Nothing in there."

And then they moved along.

CHAPTER TWENTY-EIGHT

I don't believe I've ever before felt such total despair as I felt when I heard my would-be rescuers move on. Tears ran from my eyes as I gave in to self-pity, weeping silently there in the prison that I was starting to believe would become my tomb.

I would have kept on crying, but just at that moment a mouse ran into view. Even in the dark, I could make out his features enough to see him stop to check out his unexpected guest. He stood up on his back legs and looked me over before deciding I might pose some sort of danger and darting off.

Relief flooded me now that I knew the noises I'd heard earlier were from a mouse, not a rat. I've never been particularly afraid of mice, though I'd jump and probably screech just as fast as anyone else if one startled me.

This mouse had a good bit of curiosity in him, because even though he'd run off, he was soon back, taking another look at me. He did this a few times, and then must have decided I wasn't a threat after all because he settled down and busied himself with his morning grooming session.

And, believe it or not, I actually found myself *glad* that he was there. In fact, I mentally christened him Scurry. There was something comforting in having the little guy nearby and, as odd as it sounds, I felt like he'd been *sent* to me to keep me company.

Mr. Stanley's prayer at dinner the night before (it hardly seemed possible that it had only been yesterday!) came to my mind. "*Thank you for watching over this little girl, who we all love.*" It reminded me that there would be a lot of people praying for me, and the thought brought some comfort and peace. Let me tell you, comfort and peace were two things I really needed right then. It felt as though the day would just go on and on without end.

Even with the blankets, cold penetrated through, chilling me until my teeth chattered. Thirst and hunger brought more misery as the moments and hours crept slowly by. It was the longest day of my life, even with Scurry's company. It was nice to have him there, but he wasn't much of a conversationalist.

I dozed off and on, sometimes wakened by the

maddening sound of voices nearby. Each time I'd hope more searchers were coming, but no one came near.

Nightfall came, bringing deeper cold and another wave of self-pity. I felt there was no way I could stand the total dark, and hopes of even a little warmth tormented me.

And then he was back. Jason. My captor, and yet, at that moment, my rescuer. I willed him to hurry, to get me out of there. When I heard the furniture being pulled out of the way and the floorboards being lifted, tears of gratitude swelled in my eyes.

"Hello, darling," he said. "I missed you."

He seemed to take longer than he needed to, untying the cord and helping me up out of the crawlspace. My legs felt wobbly as I stood waiting for him to put the floorboards, table, and stools back.

Then, when everything was in place again, he turned to me and very gently peeled the tape from my mouth.

"I have to use the bucket," I said bluntly. He got it, untied my hands and gave me a few moments of privacy.

"I hope you were warm enough while I was gone," he said when I'd finished and gone to sit on a stool.

"It's very cold down there," I said. "And unbelievably dark."

"I'll bring another blanket the next time I come. Should I bring a light, too?"

"No light," I said quickly, knowing he was either testing me or trying to trick me. "Someone might see it."

"I brought you more water, and some food," he said. His eyes mocked me and I knew he wasn't at all fooled by what I'd said. "Are you thirsty?"

"Yes."

"And hungry?"

"Yes."

Even though I'd said yes to both, he took his time, pausing to tell me how clever he'd been while the search went on.

"My whole family joined the search," he laughed. "I started out with a group down by the woods and then cut back, went home, and slept under my bed all day. When I heard them come in, I waited for another hour and then crept out through the basement window and 'came home,' pretending I'd gotten lost. Still, I'll probably 'help' again tomorrow because that's just the kind of guy I am."

When he'd finished bragging, Jason finally pushed a bottle of water and a sandwich wrapped in waxed paper over to me. I took a few swallows of water, controlling the urge to drain the bottle. The less I had to suffer the indignity of using that bucket, the better.

The sandwich was salami on white bread. It wasn't something I'd normally eat, but it tasted good. He offered me another one, but I shook my head.

"Thanks, but I'm full."

"You have to keep your strength up," he said, touching my face, my hair.

"For what? More nights under this shed? Is that how you treat someone you're supposed to care about?"

"Small sacrifices," he said mildly. Then, without warning, he grabbed a handful of hair and jerked my head sideways. I gasped, more in shock than pain.

"You still don't know your place," he said. His voice was angry, venomous. "Don't you understand that I *chose* you! Four nights from now — when the moon is full — I plan to make you my wife, and yet you dare speak to me that way."

"Your wife?" I repeated incredulously.

"There! See what you did? You ruined the surprise!" He stood and paced as he spoke. "Well, now you know. I don't suppose it can be helped."

"But, how ...?"

"Don't worry," he smiled indulgently, like he was humouring a child. "I've written the ceremony just for us. No one else is needed. We will take our vows together, the two of us. And then we will drink a toast to our love and drift off into that endless sleep that seals the destinies of true soulmates."

So he meant to kill me ... to kill both of us. My stomach churned with fear and nausea. Jason looked over, sighed, and shook his head.

"Don't worry. When the time comes, you will be ready," he said. "You will come with me gladly."

"And where will this, uh, ceremony be?"

"Here. Right here, my love. And now, I've waited so long, I must kiss you."

He came over, leaned down, and made good on his threat. Somehow, as repulsed as I was, I managed to kiss him back and smile when he pulled his head away.

"Our wedding night will be so special," he said huskily. I tried not to shudder.

I wondered, as the hours went by and everything he said just proved more and more that he was mad, how Jason had managed to keep it hidden up until now. And was he still carrying off a normal act when he wasn't here in the shed? I suspected he was. It was the only way he could guard his secret and keep from getting caught. Besides, he might be crazy, but he wasn't stupid. His planning had been thorough, and I couldn't think of any details he'd overlooked that might help me to get away.

I had to accept the fact that I might never leave this place alive.

"Can I leave a note for my family?" I asked.

"We shall see."

"But do I have to stay under the building when you leave? Can't you tie me somewhere up here?"

"It's not safe," he said. "But it's only for a few more

days, and then it will be over and we will be gloriously sealed together."

"The hours are so long … when you're away," I said. "Could you bring me something to help me pass the time? Something to read maybe?"

"In the *dark*?" He laughed and touched my nose with a finger playfully, like we were just a couple of friends joking around.

"Oh, right. What about an iPod or Walkman or something like that that only plays through earphones?"

He looked thoughtful. "I don't suppose there'd be any harm in that."

"Thank you, Jason," I said softly. "It will make it more bearable for me down there."

"For today, you'll have to manage," he said. "It will be light soon, and I don't have time to go home and back. I'll bring another blanket and a Walkman tomorrow. But for now, you know what we have to do."

I stood up. As much as I dreaded spending another twelve hours or more in the crawlspace, I was determined not to fight it.

Chapter Twenty-Nine

I made up my mind to relax and sleep as much as possible the second day I was in the crawlspace. Even so, it was hard to stay calm. Thoughts of my parents tore into my heart. I knew they were suffering as much as I was, though in a different way. I tried not to think of them too much, but sometimes I couldn't help it. I knew they'd be out of their minds with worry and grief, and it only added to my misery.

And Greg. What was he thinking? I knew he'd be frantic and worried, no matter what had happened between us.

Once, just once, I let myself fantasize about being free and seeing Greg somewhere. I played it out in my head. We'd hug and kiss and everything would be all right.

Only, that just made me feel worse. My chest hurt and tears spilled out and I had to tell myself *very* sternly not to do that again.

I found myself still wide awake when daylight came, which made me realize why I was having difficulty falling asleep, in spite of my fatigue.

My whole system was thrown off by the reversal of sleep and wake times! All of a sudden I was forced to stay up during the nights — when Jason showed up — and sleep during the daytime. Not that the light was a problem by any means, since so little of it filtered in between the boards. Still, it was enough for me to see dimly once my eyes adjusted.

It was only completely dark down there when I first went in — before the sun came up — and again later on after it went down. But at least then I knew that Jason would be coming along. He moved under cover of darkness, and now he didn't even have to worry about his footprints. With all the searchers that had been around, no one would think anything of track marks, wherever they went. He'd laughed about the tracks up to the shed's door, telling me he no longer had to worry about brushing his away with branches. I understood then what the whishing sounds were that I'd heard the first time he left me, and it actually angered me that I hadn't figured out something that simple.

No doubt my difficulty sleeping also had a lot to do with the fact that I now knew Jason meant to kill me. That's not the kind of thing you can just put out of your mind. But I did my best by telling myself over and over that I *would* escape somehow.

And then, of course, when I did manage to sleep, it was fitful and light. I woke a number of times to the sounds of Scurry scampering around, and also when voices or footsteps were near enough for me to hear them.

It was torturous, knowing that help was so close and being completely unable to do anything about it.

Thankfully, it seemed a bit warmer down there this time, and I think I managed to sleep more than I had the day before. It helped the time go by faster, and when the light faded I found myself looking forward to Jason's arrival. When he came, it seemed much later than it had the night before.

He was in a bad mood, grumbling about having to go to school all day and not getting enough sleep afterward. I could barely keep myself from snapping that it was probably better than spending twelve or fourteen hours under the shed.

After relieving myself and having some water and a sandwich (today's was peanut butter), I was treated to more hours of listening to Jason's plans. He told me that he'd be bringing me a "bridal gown" for the ceremony.

"It would sure be nice to have a shower first," I hinted. As expected, he ignored the comment and just went on about how he'd bought the so-called gown pretending it was for his mom for Christmas.

"A bridal gown for your *mom?*" I said, unable to keep the disbelief from my voice.

"Well, it's actually a nightgown and housecoat," he admitted, "but it's all white and flowing. It'll be perfect, you'll see. I can't bring it here until the big night, though, because there's nowhere to hide it up here, and," he nodded toward the floorboards, "we wouldn't want it to get dirty down there."

No, but it's fine for *me* to be stuck down there in the dirt, I thought. Outwardly, I nodded solemnly, like he'd just made a very good point.

He talked on and on about the "wedding night." As you can imagine, I found it a bit difficult to look thrilled and excited about what he was describing. Vows he'd written for us to say to each other, food he'd bring for our "wedding feast," and the "special" champagne. On and on he went. Crazy details, disjointed thoughts ... all nonsense, but all the more dangerous because they made perfect sense in his twisted mind.

"I almost forgot to tell you about the music!" he said, clapping his hands together. "I've burned a special CD for us with just the right songs. Just wait until you hear them."

I smiled.

"Oh, that reminds me. I brought a Walkman for you, like you asked." He reached into the bag of supplies, a lot of it junk food that he snacked on all night, and pulled out the Walkman. "I thought about bringing our wedding CD, but then it wouldn't be special for just that night. Anyway, there are only a couple of CDs with it, so you'll get some repetition."

"That doesn't matter. Anything at all will be an improvement over laying there listening to nothing." Another smile — I felt like my face would crack soon. "Thank you, Jason. And, could I ask for one more thing?"

"What?"

"A toothbrush and toothpaste?" I forced a little laugh and added, "I guess that was two things, wasn't it? But anyway, I'd sure like to be able to brush my teeth."

"No problem," he said. "I'll bring them tomorrow night. And now, as much as I hate to leave you, I've *got* to get home and try to grab a couple of hours sleep before school."

"I understand." More time in the hole, but I decided even that was better than having to sit there and keep listening to him rave. I stood compliantly while he went through the routine of moving the floorboards, tying me, and taping my mouth. Then he lifted me down into the crawlspace, put the earphones on me, and positioned the Walkman where I could reach it to turn it on and off, or change CDs.

In no time, he'd put everything back in place and I heard him go out the door. It would be hours before sunrise and more than that before anyone might happen along. I closed my eyes and said a short prayer.

If Jason had his way, I had two more days to live.

CHAPTER THIRTY

Thinking about it, I don't know how I made myself wait. No doubt it was fear: fear that the plan I'd formulated on the first night I'd spent as a prisoner under the shed's floor wouldn't work.

It was well after daylight broke before I made a move. Scurry was sitting in his usual place — I told myself he'd come to like having me there — and the movement startled him, making him run off. I made a silent promise that, if I got out of there alive, I'd come back and bring him some jelly beans. I'd heard mice like them better than cheese.

Even though my fingers were loose it was difficult to do anything with my wrists tied. I fumbled a few times, but was careful not to rush. A single mistake could ruin everything.

It all had to be done by feel, of course, but as I

made progress I found my heartbeat quickening with excitement. They felt right! Until I had them in my hand, there'd been no way to know whether or not the batteries from the Walkman would fit my alarm.

Using my fingers, I explored the cavity to make sure I was getting the right ends on the positive posts, and then I inserted the batteries into the alarm.

Then came the nerve-wracking wait for someone — anyone — to come near enough to the shed. It was possible that the alarm wouldn't work after being slammed down hard enough to bust the battery door and crack the case, but I didn't test it. Maybe that was fear again, though I told myself I wasn't wasting one second of power from the batteries. Since I didn't know how much charge was in them, I couldn't risk draining them before the sounds of the alarm could summon help.

It felt like ten hours, but it was probably only one or two, before I heard voices. Kids! I hesitated, wondering if I should wait for someone older, but then I remembered how curious kids are. I felt sure they'd come to see what was going on — if the alarm worked — but what they'd do afterward remained to be seen.

Heart pounding, my finger moved and clicked the switch. The siren came to life immediately, blaring in what was an unbelievably loud sound in the confines of the crawlspace.

It wasn't two minutes before I heard the sounds I was praying for: feet pounding on the steps, banging, and voices. As much as I wanted to know what they were saying, I didn't dare turn off the alarm as long as they were there.

They banged on the door a few times, but any other sounds they made were drowned out by the siren, in spite of how hard I strained to hear. Then there was nothing, and I knew they were gone. I switched the alarm off to save the batteries.

"Please let them get help," I prayed. And I prepared myself to wait, either for them to come back with an adult, or for someone else to come along. I knew it could be a while, so it was a surprise when I heard footsteps again after what seemed no more than ten minutes.

I could tell at once that the sounds I now heard were from adults. As they reached the shed, I switched the alarm on again and over the screeching noise it made, I heard an excited shout.

It blurs after that. A crashing sound, heavy footsteps on the floor above me. I turned the alarm off again and kicked at the floorboards with all my might. I heard scraping when the table and stools were moved and then light flooded in as the boards were lifted out.

"It's her!"

There, leaning down, reaching down, pulling me up and out, was Officer Mueller. Beside him, Officer

Stanton stood with tears running down her cheeks. Well, to be honest, we were all crying.

"My parents," I said, the second the tape was off my mouth.

"I was calling it in while he was getting you out of there," Stanton said.

They both worked on getting the ties off me, and in no time I was completely freed. You have no idea how good it felt to be able to walk and move normally again, or how good it felt a few moments later when they led me out of the building and, for the first time since my horror began, I was outside again.

"Who are we after?" Mueller asked as they helped me to the cruiser.

"Jason Puckett. He's probably at school right now."

"We need to pick him up before he hears that you're out," Stanton said. Now that her tears were dried, she couldn't stop smiling. It was quite a contrast from the officer I'd first met — the woman who'd been so cool and professional. I decided I liked her just fine either way.

"And Eric? He's innocent, you know."

"Yes, we know. He's already been released. When you disappeared, we took a harder look at some of the evidence."

"Like the height of the person on the surveillance tape?"

"We caught that later. First thing we discovered was the complete absence of fingerprints on the sheets of paper that were planted at his place. Since some of them were just drafts of the letter that was sent to you, it didn't make sense he'd be that careful about prints."

We were nearing my place by then and I saw my mom in the doorway. As we pulled into the drive she hurried out and the next moment she was holding me and sobbing.

"If *I* went outside in this weather with no jacket on, *I'd* be in trouble," I said teasingly. And then I broke down, too.

Dad arrived minutes later and the whole emotional scene was repeated. He'd continued searching with the volunteers while Mom had been asked to remain at home in case the culprit called. She said it was much worse having to stay in the house when all she could think was that she should be *doing* something.

A lot more things happened that day. Some of them kind of jumble together, but a few stand out.

Like Betts's face when she came running into my kitchen after she'd heard the news and rushed over.

Like hearing that Jason had been arrested and that the Crown had already decided to ask that he be charged as an adult. This was no longer a case of stalking; it was kidnapping, unlawful confinement, and a bunch of other things. Jason was going to be locked away for a long, long time.

EYES OF A STALKER

Like calling Eric and telling him how sorry I was for what he'd been through. He said he knew it wasn't my fault and he didn't hold anything against me for believing he was a stalker, even for a little while, but I think he's over his crush on me for good.

Like sitting in the kitchen after a lovely, hot shower, dressed in clean clothes and eating a steaming hot bowl of soup and then hearing the kitchen door open and looking up …

And seeing Greg there.

Chapter Thirty-One

Normally, I'd have sat and waited to see what he wanted, but there was nothing normal about the last few days. I got up and went to him, put my arms around him, and felt my heart lift with joy as his encircled me.

I didn't care if I had to swallow my pride or not. It spilled out of me — all of it. Why I'd broken up with him, how much I'd missed him, everything.

At first he just held me and didn't say anything. I realized after a few minutes that was because he was too choked up to speak. When he did finally speak, he just kept saying, "I love you, Shelby. You *know* I love you."

"I love you too," I said, feeling this huge surge of joy. "And I don't even care about you going out with Tina."

"Going out with Tina?" He pulled back, his face astonished. "What are you talking about?"

"Tyrone's party. You were there with her."

"With Tina? No way! She asked me, but I told her no. I mean, there's nothing wrong with her, but …"

His voice trailed off for a moment and then I could see him sorting through it. "You thought that, because she was beside me, we were together. To be honest, it was getting on my nerves how every time I turned around it seemed she was there. But I never thought anyone — least of all you — would think we were there *together*."

I felt a little embarrassed for listening to Betts. I could see exactly what had happened! She'd heard something about Tina asking Greg to go with her, and passed it on to me as if it was a done deal.

"I should have known," I said. "I should have known you better than that. If I had, none of what happened … I mean, I'd have …"

I almost didn't know what I was trying to say, but it didn't matter. It was all over.

"Anyway, didn't you understand the story I wrote for you?"

"What story?" I asked.

"The one about the whooping cranes."

"I remember you reading it. It was really nice." I looked up and saw him smiling in a sweet, patient way, like he does when I'm slow clueing in to something. "Why? Is there something special about whooping cranes?"

"*I* think so." He leaned down and kissed me. "Once they choose a mate, they stay together for life."

ACKNOWLEDGEMENTS

As always, I am indebted to those whose support and encouragement have made my dream a reality.

My husband, partner, and best friend, Brent. I love you truly, madly, deeply.

My parents, Bob and Pauline Russell.

My son Anthony, his wife, Maria, and daughters Emilee and Ericka. My daughter Pamela and her husband, David Jardine. My brothers and their families: Danny and Gail; Andrew, Shelley, and Bryce. My "other" family: Ron and Phoebe Sherrard, Ron Sherrard and Dr. Kiran Pure, Bruce and Roxanne Mullin, and Karen Sherrard.

Friends: Janet Aube, Jimmy Allain, Karen Arseneault, Dawn Black, Karen Donovan, Angi Garofolo, John Hambrook, Sandra Henderson, Jim Hennessy, Alf Lower, Mary Matchett, Johnnye Montgomery, Marsha Skrypuch, Linda Stevens, Ashley Smith, Pam Sturgeon,

Paul Theriault and Bonnie Thompson.

At The Dundurn Group: Kirk Howard, Publisher, and the whole team, particularly my awesome editor, Barry Jowett, and director of design, Jennifer Scott. Also, special thanks to Alison Carr for her work on the cover, and Dan Wagstaff for maintaining good humour no matter how much I pestered him.

My fabulous agent, Leona Trainer of Transatlantic Literary Agency.

Teenagers! Hearing from you is the *best* part of writing, and I love getting your letters and emails. You are on these pages and they belong to you.

Very special thanks to readers Elizabeth Foran and Kirsti McNabney. Your project was amazing and the slideshow was awesome!